To Dianne Hess—
with appreciation and love

Virginia
1863

I have been told to keep a record of what we do, tho I do not know why I was picked. I am not the best at spelling. Coreper — Corporal Bell is. I am not the smartest, either. Osgood Tracy is the smartest in the Company. That is why we call him the Little Profeser. And we are doing exactly what we have been doing for some days now — marching around and getting nowhere! Besides, keeping this record has already been the death of two good men and I don't need more bad luck on my head! Well, you have read it all.

Luten — Lieutenant Toms looked over what I wrote and said I had got it all wrong and to do it again. "Put in details," he said, so I will. Lieutenant Alexander Toms has ordered me to keep "an accurate and honest account" of G Company of the 122nd Regiment, New York Volunteers, from Onondaga County in New York State. Lt. Toms is keeping his own account and will combine it with this at the end of the war to make "a true and fair history of our brave men and their core — courageous deeds." That is exactly his words. I still do not see why I have to keep this record when I know it will be my death.

Lt. Toms said to stop complaining like a greenhorn recruit. He said I was chosen because he can read my handwriting easier than most. He also said there is no curse to keeping this journal and that he is pretty certain I will last to the end of this war to finish it — unlike the first two. "You are not one of those crazy patriot fools who sticks his head up high to show how brave you are," he said. "When we come under fire, you hug the ground like a baby hugs its mother's teat." I want it clear that I am as good a soldier as any in G Company and have a torn-up arm and a black tooth to prove it!

Lt. Toms said what I wrote was better, but was still missing some important details. When I talked back fresh and said, "But I put your name in as many times as I could, sir," he said I could sit apart and miss dinner til I know what I left out. This is hard to do because we had scared up some hens who are now in a pot with some turnips and an onion and the smell makes my head swim.

What I remember is that last month — which was October — we left Warrenton Junction and went north to Bristoe Station, then on to Centreville — all in Virginia — to head off the Rebs, who was trying to get at the National Capital in Washington. The fighting was hot but we saw little of it, as we was assigned to protect the rear of the supply train as usual. Our army pushed the Rebs back and back and then we followed them south and are today close by Rappahannock Station — still in the Secessia land of Virginia. So marching has been our work and entertainment now for almost twenty days. I will add only that the first keeper of this journal was killed on the march to Gettysburg by a runaway wagon; the second died at the hands of a sharpshooter on a very peaceful Sabbath — the only shot fired that day that I recall and the only man killed in the army. What else is there to say?

Lt. Toms said there was more to say and that I should "think carefully and fully." But how can I when all around me is the smell of chicken and the sound of smacking lips? I will try this: G Company is forty-two strong today, plus one three-legged dog and one Negro camp servant. We have had nine desertions since Gettysburg, so tomorrow there may be fewer. It is November 5, 1863.

I did not show this to the Lt. Instead I asked the Little Profeser to read it and he did, but he could not talk because his mouth was full. He did point to a written "I" and when I looked puzzled he pointed to me. I am not as bright as some, but I am not an empty barrel, either. So I will write: *My name is James Edmond Pease.* I am a private in the United States Army of the Potomac, which is under the command of General George Meade, and I am sixteen years old, I think, or thereabouts.

I showed this to Lt. Toms and he smiled and said, "Pull up a log, Private Pease. While you sup, I will tell you some other things I would like in the journal." And that is what I am going to do — tho there is mighty little chicken left to "sup" on!

November 6

Lt. Toms's first bit of advice was "start with the date and the rest will follow naturally." So I have given the date and will add that we was up at five this morning, marching by six, with only hardtack biscuits and a tin of coffee in between. The coffee had to be as old as Colonel Titus himself and tasted like the inside of a boot with the foot still inside. But since it was an improvement over yesterday's coffee, I am not complaining.

Once again our orders from regimental head-quarters are to guard the rear of the supply train. This is as good a job as any to me, but does not sit well with the rest of the men, who are eager to see some fighting. And once again Lt. Toms has sent Willie Dodd and his dog, Spirit, with a request that we be allowed to join up with the rest of the 122nd—at the forward line of battle!

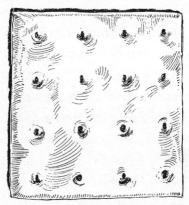

Decided to draw our ever-present "friend" and, after several attempts, managed to produce this version of a hardtack biscuit. Johnny Henderson said it looked like a real tooth-breaker to him — which I take to be a compliment.

At noon of the same day

The answer to Lt. Toms's request was no—as it has been every day since Gettysburg. I did sigh with relief when I heard this, but I also know that my bad luck can follow me into a church if it wants, so there is no relaxing for me.

After this, we marched along for four miles in a cold drizzle that has left us damp and cranky, me especially since I am sure every Reb sharpshooter has me as a target. Even Johnny Henderson—who usually has a smile painted on his face—said he would bite the ear off of any man or beast who looked cross-eyed at him. Charlie Shelp said Johnny was just missing his mama again, so Johnny went at him and the two rolled around on the ground, fists and mud flying and cussing and such, with the rest of the Company and several of the mule-drivers looking on. I may be mistaken, but I believe the Company's sentiment was with Johnny, as Charlie has offended about everyone with his mouth. He did me when he started calling me Orphan Boy.

One of the officers of the supply train, Major Mitchell, rode up just as Lt. Toms was pulling the two apart. The Major told Johnny and Charlie to "save your fight for the Rebels," but it was Lt. Toms who answered: "We are saving it, but guarding a mule's ass is not our notion of a fight." Major Mitchell looked as if he had drunk bad milk and said, "Lieutenant Toms, if anyone would have you, I would be happy to see you get your wish," and then rode off. How is it that when Lt. Toms talks back nothing happens to him, but when I do I get to sit aside and watch everyone else eat? And he did not even say "sir," that I heard.

3 o'clock

The supply train has been stopped a-while, so I will do some writing, as instructed. Lt. Toms wants me to do a list of all the men in our company, being careful to give their proper ages and spell all names correctly. This is not such a hard task since our Company is down considerable from its original 97 men and 3 officers. Here are those left:

Lieutenant Alexander Toms 43

Sergeant Robert Donoghue 26

Corporal John Bell 21	Corporal Philip Drake 22
Private James Pease 16	Pte. David Bernard 20
Pte. John Keller 22	Pte. Charles Stevens 31
Pte. Develois Stevens 17	Pte. William Kittler 26
Pte. Philo Olmstead 35	Pte. James Crozier 21
Pte. Charles Holman 37	Pte. Benjamin Breed 21
Pte. William Bateman 18	Pte. Niles Rogers 34
Pte. Charlie Shelp 25	Pte. Theodore Stevens 16
Pte. Lyman Swim 17	Pte. Osgood Tracy 21
Pte. Hiram Wicks 29	Pte. William Zellers 30
Pte. Chester Youngs 21	Pte. Jehial Lamphier 44
Pte. Cornelius Mahar 20	Pte. Peter McQuade 17
Pte. Miles McGough 22	Pte. Sanford Van Dyke 18
Pte. John Williams 31	Pte. Henry Wyatt 17
Pte. Henry Clements 18	Pte. Hiram Woolsey 20
Pte. George Chittenden 29	Pte. James Wyatt 20
Pte. Alonzo Clute 20	Pte. Brower Davis 19
Pte. John Doty 35	Pte. John Farner 44

Pte. Miles Gorham 21   Pte. Boswell Grant 38
Pte. Will Hammond 17   Pte. Johnny Henderson 19
Pte. Joseph Landphier 34
      Ptc. Willie Dodd 16   Spirit 3

We have no capt. since Lt. Toms was reduced in rank, no second lt. since Harrison Jilson died of typhus fever, and no third lt. since Ernst Altgelt was transferred to K Company after all their officers was killed. Lt. Toms has a Negro servant named Caesar, who was freed from a house here in Virginia and works for his keep. He does not know how old he is, but Lt. Toms guesses he might be as old as 50. That is all of them every one, unless one is in the woods on a call of nature and I have forgotten him.

Same day near dark
Skirmish fire off to our right a mile or so. Firing came on very suddenly and is very hot. We are so used to hearing cannon and musket fire that we hardly notice it any-more, but this time it sounded sharper to me and I got gooseflesh when I knew it was getting closer. Lt. Toms thinks the Rebs are driving in our guard pickets and told us to load our muskets and form a line along the road to face the oncoming sound.

Everyone—including Lt. Toms—looks nervous. "Hold your fire, boys. Hold your fire," Lt. Toms is barking out louder than he needs to. "Hold your fire til I give the command." The Lt. and some others may be recalling Gettysburg, but I think most of the men are nervous because we was issued only five rounds of ammunition today—ammunition being in short supply—and five rounds will not last but a breath or two in a good fight. Lt. Toms has just screamed, "What the Devil are you doing, Pease?" and I told him I was making "an accurate and honest account of the fight, as ordered, sir." "Load your damned musket and find a place in line!" he ordered very loudly, which I will do now.

Later

It turned out to be all noise and excitement and nothing more for us—which is fine, since I am not eager to add my blood to the cover of this book. Not for $13 a month, which we haven't seen in three months any-way!

The fighting came very close—maybe a half mile off—and went on for several minutes. We could hear the *pop, pop, popping* of muskets talking to each other and even smell the burnt-up powder drifting through the trees, but it is very hilly in here so we did not see anything at all even with most of the leaves gone.

Major Mitchell rode up and told Lt. Toms to take us out a quarter of a mile from the road and form another line of defense there. We was to hold off the enemy while he moved his wagons to a safer spot. We responded instantly, but had got only a few steps when Major Mitchell called out, "And, Lt. Toms. Do not fire til you see the enemy clearly, do you understand?" Lt. Toms said, "Yes, sir," but I could see he wanted to say more. And so did the rest of us.

What happened at Gettysburg was a mistake. A terrible mistake, but an honest one. The smoke from thousands of muskets and the hours-long cannon duel was choking thick and blinding. I know, because I was behind our breastworks of cut saplings, and I saw those hazy sillouet—silhouettes of men coming up the hill—dark, ghostlike shapes without definition and, I might add, without a regimental flag either. What I did see plainly was that they was firing at us—just like any good Reb would.

I hadn't been in many fights before Gettysburg—none of us had—and I wasn't a very good shot either. I just pulled the trigger and hoped to hit a tree or something close enough to a Reb to scare him off. They was the enemy, but I figured that if they didn't try to hurt me, I didn't have to hurt them. But something happened at Gettysburg that changed that.

First, like a fool I stuck my head up to see what the Rebs was up to and saw those soldiers coming at us. Before I had a chance to get down behind cover, a minié ball ripped into my arm. It wasn't bad—just a grazing—but it burned as hot as a poker. Then while I was sitting there looking at my arm and the little bit of blood that was oozing out, a shell exploded above us and I got hit in the mouth by a piece of flying iron. I was so mad I jumped up and fired back—this time taking better aim. The rest of the Company fired at those advancing figures, too, til we had silenced those guns, every one of them. It was what we had been told and taught to do, after all, and no one who was there would have ever blamed us. We never knew they was Union soldiers til it was all over!

Only, the officers at head-quarters wasn't there and did not understand how we could fire at our own men when they was so close. They said our Company had panicked because it was our first real fight and that Lt. Toms had failed to control us—which is just not true, neither one. No one believed Lt. Toms's story, and all the other officers who had been near us and could have told the truth was either dead or wounded. Of course, I blamed myself some for what happened to the Lt., me being unlucky and all from birth.

That is why we all wanted to say something to Major Mitchell, but no one did. We know better than to do that when there is a real fight going on. Instead we went out to welcome the Rebs, and I think we was all in a mood for a good fight. Even me! But before we got very far, there was a ferocious volley of musketry up ahead, followed by a loud cheer.

"Those will be our reinforcements," Lt. Toms said, and I believe he was disappointed that we had not been there to help. The fighting was pretty fierce for a few minutes; then, very quickly, it began to let up and started drifting away from us til we was standing in a quiet patch of woods with nothing but the smell of the powder to remind us why we was there. Lt. Toms had us form a defensive line any-way and we stayed like that in the empty woods, mostly watching Spirit chase after tossed sticks. Major Mitchell remembered us three hours later and sent word that we could come back in, which we did promptly.

Lt. Toms saw me writing and asked to see it. He said I got it pretty much right except that he had not been nervous and had not been thinking about Gettysburg at all til the Major said what he said. He added that for someone who did not want to keep the Company journal I was certainly scribbling an awful lot down, so maybe I enjoyed this more than I let on. He is right about this last, any-way.

November 7

Received our orders this morning: Guard rear of supply train, et cetera, et cetera and so forth. Lt. Toms accepted the orders as he always does, with a crisp salute to the delivering captain and a polite "Yes, sir." But when the Capt. was gone, Lt. Toms let out such a blast of cussing and yelling and stomping about that even the mule-drivers nearby was greatly impressed. Heavy artillery duel way off and exchanges of musket fire. Some are in the middle of it today, but not us.

The Lt. said that when things are quiet, I am to write "brief histories of each of the men." A battle is going on, but the supply wagons hardly move during a fight, so there is not much to do. The Lt. also said I should start with myself, and I will do as ordered and be done with it.

I have no recollection of my parents, not one, tho Uncle often complained that the Angel of Death had freed them of their burden and saddled him with it instead, so I guess they both died of fever or some such. I was brought up by Uncle and Aunt—they did not like me using their given names and so I don't—on their farm near the town of Warners, which is not near anything at all, and my earliest recollection is of clearing rocks from the field while Uncle plowed. "Prayer will bring you to Heaven's path and work will guide your footsteps" was a favorite phrase of Uncle, and he practiced what he preached seven days a week, taking but a few minutes off to pray on the Sabbath. When we wasn't doing chores, I copied or read passages from the Bible, old newspapers, and the three books we had. Of my aunt, I do not remember much other than she rarely left the house, rarely spoke—and when she did, her voice was as frail as a flower's petal—and seemed to be always nervous.

I guess I would be there still except that the rain did not fall as expected in the summer of 1862 and we seemed to produce more rocks than vegetables. Uncle began quoting the Bible more and more and Aunt seemed even more uneasy—if that is possible—and both of them turned cold eyes on me as less and less food made its way to the table. They never did say it, but I think they blamed me for holding back the rain! Maybe they was right. I mean, I was bad luck for my parents, so who knows about such things?

So one morning, to escape the stares, I went out and sat in the woods by the edge of the field. My thought was to join Uncle when he came out to work, only a strange thing happened. As I sat there, Uncle and Aunt began doing their usual chores—milking the goat, feeding the few chickens left, repairing a broken fence and so forth—and neither so much as looked up for me or called my name. All day I watched and all day they

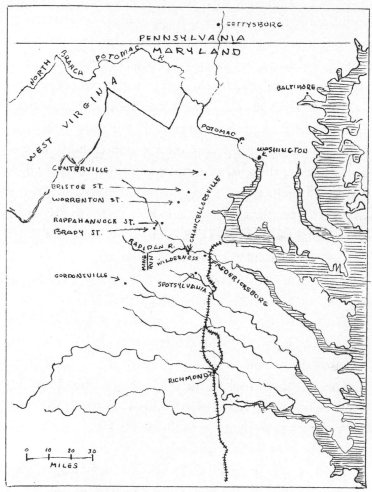

Drew this map of some of the places we have visited or might visit — according to Sgt. Donoghue. Johnny said I should have put little waves where the water is instead of straight lines; the Little Profeser said I should have put in the locations of mountains and lakes; the Lt. thought it nice, but said that Baltimore was closer to Washington than I have shown. I think some-one else should draw the map next time!

went about their business. I was hungry at lunch and hungrier still at supper, but I did not budge. And they did not call for me or in any way seem to miss me. Even then I kept hoping for some sort of sign from them. The sun went down, and a while after this the yellow light from the house candles was snuffed out and it was clear they had gone to sleep. Which was sign enough for me. So I started walking down the road, taking away the one burden of theirs that I could. I continued walking til the day, three months later, when I saw a call to a war meeting and signed on as part of G Company. And that is my story told in more words than it deserves.

Later

A surprise. We was ordered forward in the afternoon to support the actions of the rest of the 122nd. Lt. Toms and some others looked happy with this, but I am not alone when I say that I was content to guard the supply train, as there is little to dodge back there but mule droppings.

We was issued three days' rations and forty rounds of ammunition—so we knew we would be very close to the fighting—then off we marched, joining up with several other companies along the way. My knapsack never felt so heavy as on that short walk.

We followed the road for five miles or so, but as we got close to the sounds of fighting, we went to the right and crossed a field with a sorry-looking farmhouse sitting in the middle. The owners — a sour old man and his sour old wife — stood in the doorway watching us file by. She was saying over and over, "Yank murd'rers. Yu'll burn 'n Hell," tho she changed it every so often to "Thivin' murd'rin' Yanks. Burn 'n Hell, all a ya!" The man just glowered at us and spit wads of drippy brown tobacca juice in our direction. Charlie Shelp talked back to them mean, but such comes natural to Charlie. The rest of us was just happy to get to the woods so those two ancients could not put the evil-eye on our backs. I certainly did not need any more of that trailing after me!

It didn't take long before I saw signs of the fight — trees with their sides chewed at by musket balls, chunks of earth ripped up by ten-pound Parrott shells. On a little, we passed some trees that had been cut in half, as if a giant clumsy hand had snapped off the tops and tossed them aside. Then we came to the first dead soldier — a Reb in a crisp new butternut uniform.

He was sitting on the ground, leaning back against a tree, and seemed to be in a comfortable position with his eyes closed and his hands clasped together on his lap. Any other time, I would have thought him asleep and dreaming of home and peach pie, but out here that thought does not scour. Besides, his face was already the color of yellow clay and the front of his new uniform was stained dark with blood.

"Shot thru the heart clean," the Little Profeser said as he stood over the body. "Dead since morning by his looks." "Not dead soon enough for me," Shelp added, and then he turned to me and said, "Hey, Orphan Boy. This one here looks like you. Got a cowlick the same as you, too." And he was right. The dead soldier even looked to be my age, which did not help my confidence any. "Move along. Move along," Lt. Toms ordered us. "There are plenty more Rebels up ahead and they'll be alive to shoot back."

We didn't see any more bodies, ours or theirs, so I guess both sides had time to haul away their dead and wounded. Except the boy, that is. Up ahead was a wide-open field where we formed a line of battle along one side after leaving our knapsacks and Spirit in the care of Caesar. Across the field from us—maybe 300 yards away—was another thick, dark woods in which the Rebs was supposed to be hiding. The field was pretty well churned up by the earlier fighting, with the stiff bodies of fifteen or twenty horses and a lot of equipment scattered all about. So we stayed there—500 soldiers shoulder to shoulder with muskets cocked and at the ready—waiting and waiting for their charge.

For the better part of the day we was on that cold ground, muskets aimed at the invisible enemy, and listening to the real battle going on somewhere far away to our left. Some of the boys wanted to get the fight going and called out to the Rebs to come on and such, which is a silly thing to do as far as I am concerned. If a fight is going to happen, it will happen and doesn't need me to hurry it along. It wasn't long before the cold got into my bones and set me off shivering, so I put my hands in my pockets and prayed that this would not mean another round of my ague. The last time I had those shivering night-sweats, I thought I might die I was so weak and tired. After the sun set, a courier appeared with fresh orders, and a few minutes later Lt. Toms said, "Okay, boys, we are going back."

The Reb boy was still there, leaning back and, like a good soldier, waiting his turn to be collected. And the sour old man and sour old woman was there waiting for us. Everybody waits in a war.

*Charlie Shelp on a day when he seemed unusually pleasant and cheerful —
for him! Lt. Toms said the drawing wasn't bad and that I could include others if I had time.*

November 8

Today's orders: guard the rear of the wagons — so I guess yesterday was a real emergency and no one will have us yet. Lt. Toms did not get upset today and he did not send Willie and Spirit out with his usual request. "It would be kinder for them to shoot me and be done with it," he said quietly, and I think he meant it. He went on to say that he couldn't go home with this disgrace on his head, and since they wouldn't let him fight he could never prove himself in battle. It did not help that Lt. Clapp from A Company visited this morning at breakfast and told Lt. Toms about the fighting they had done yesterday while we was guarding an empty field.

Later

I asked Sgt. Donoghue what I should write down as his history and he gave me the queerest look. When I said it was an order from the Lt., he shook his head and said it was all non-sense, this writing down what happened and who was there and such. But then he said, "My father was in the regular army when I was born, and my mother and I and later my two younger brothers, we all followed him when he moved from place to place. He was a cooper by trade, and a fine one, too, but no one outside would hire the Irish, so that is how he came to the army. His name was Flann, and hers was Mary. Have you got all of this, because I don't want to say it again. When I could, I joined the army, which is why I am here. Is that enough?" I said yes and he walked away muttering, "Non-sense, that is all it is," and I was happy to have gotten what I did from him. I will add that the Sgt. is married and has three children, all girls.

I am still free of the ague, so I guess it has passed me by this time.

November 9

Much the same "excitement" as yesterday—following the wagons. When we stopped, I was sent out with some others to watch for enemy raiders who might sneak up on our wagons. Spent most of the time wrapped up in my poncho facing away from an icy wind and thinking about that dead Reb boy. I wondered if he would get a proper burial or whether he would just sit out there til some hungry pig found him. And I wondered if his friends missed him or if his parents was somewhere thinking about him and worrying. Then I thought, at least he had someone to worry after him, which made the wind feel even sharper and me feel very lonely indeed.

7 o'clock

Talk tonight at supper was about the elections and my curse. I am too young to vote, so I did not listen closely to what was said about the election. I do know that all who could voted against Copperhead candidates, who are for the secession of the South. My curse was another story.

Most—the Little Profeser among them—said such things do not exist, except in the mind of the unlucky, and Charlie Shelp added that I was as dumb as a fence post for believing such things. Everyone laughed at that and I felt my face flush red, but Johnny Henderson jumped in then and said it was dangerous to make fun of a curse. He said his uncle once spit down a neighbor's well and the next day his uncle drowned while fishing. "He'd fished that pond for thirty, forty years," Johnny said, "but he'd put bad luck on himself by spitting down that well, and the water got him!"

Shelp said Johnny was as stupid as me, and that together we had as much sense as a drum. But I wasn't listening to Shelp; I was smiling at Johnny, because I knew he had made up the story so Shelp wouldn't pick on me alone. It didn't even bother me much when Shelp made up a song about me and sang it over and over:

Good people, I will sing you a ditty,
And hope that it doesn't annoy;

I make an appeal to your pity,
For I'm an unfortunate boy.
'Twas under an unlucky planet
That I was born one night;
My life since first I began it
Has been cursed in dark and light.
So do not make sport of my troubles,
But pity one who feels no joy,
For I'm an uncomfortable, horrible, terrible,
*   inconsolable Jonah Boy.*

November 10

Crossed the Rappahannock on a pontoon bridge at the tail end of the wagon train. Since there must be 500 wagons in the train, we did not get to cross til it was nearly dark. It is a good thing we didn't have to wait for the cattle to cross, too! Lt. Toms seems all in and is not his usual self, which might have something to do with the official report that was circulated yesterday. It congratulated the 122nd for charging and carrying a strong enemy position during the battle of the seventh, and for taking 1,600 prisoners, plus small arms and three cannons. It also said that Lt. Clapp had been promoted to the rank of captain because of his valor and leadership in the field. Some of the Company have been trying to think of a way to cheer up Lt. Toms, but so far we have had no good ideas.

November 11

Today the trampling of thousands of cavalry horses, followed by tens of thousands of foot soldiers, followed by thousands of mules and hundreds of wagons, churned the road into a mud-pike. Spent too much time hauling stuck wagons from the thick soup.

At one point we came to a wagon whose six mules had gotten tired and stopped to rest. The driver was heaping one cuss after another on them, along with some fierce blows from his whip, but they just stood there with heads bowed. Willie—who has a tender spot for all dumb creatures, not just three-legged ones—told the driver to stop what he was doing, which the driver did, but only so he could turn his mortar-gun mouth on Willie and the rest of us nearby.

While the driver's back was turned, the mules ended their rest break and began walking forward very slowly. The driver never even heard them—not with his mouth firing cusses, Willie answering back, and Spirit dancing around barking. And, of course, no one—not even his fellow drivers!—bothered to tell him what was happening. It wasn't til an officer from the supply train asked the driver where his wagon was that he realized it was gone. At least twenty wagons had already passed by, so the driver raced off after his own, slipping and sliding in the mud while throwing more cusses back at us. It was a fine spectacle to watch and gave the boys a needed laugh.

Several of the boys are sick with the ague and flux and had to report to the doctors, but so far I am fine. There is a rumor that the paymaster is near and this has raised the hopes of some—including me—who wish to visit the sutler for supplies. We have had nothing but shelled corn, a little meat, hardtack, and coffee for three days now.

Later

Lt. Toms very quiet today and no one bothered him with talk. So when Henry Wyatt wanted to know where we was headed, he asked his brother James—Henry being shy always. James asked Corp. Bell, who asked Sgt. Donoghue, who, after some thought and hesitation, went to Lt. Toms and stated Henry's question. "Where are we going!" Lt. Toms shouted. "How in the name of Hell would I know? They don't tell me any-thing any-more! The damned mules know more than I do! Ask them!" Lt. Toms fell quiet again, and Sgt. Donoghue came over to us and said we could ask our own damned questions after this. The rumor about the paymaster turned out to be just that. No pay — no trip to the sutler.

November 12

We are headed for Brandy Station, where the army will spend the winter. This information was gotten from one of the mule-drivers. Johnny Henderson thinks this is about as close to actually talking to a mule as you can get, a mule being a rather more reliable source of information than a driver. The rest of the day had us marching, hauling stuck wagons, marching, hauling, marching, hauling — and a sorry, muddy bunch we were by night.

I have a case of the shakes, which may be the ague or something worse, and have been having trouble sleeping. I have also had a hard time forgetting that dead Reb boy. I am going to take quinine and hope this will drive off the ague and the boy.

November 19

We have been in camp this week, getting ready for winter. By the time we got here, most of the men had already chosen their tent-mates for the cold months ahead. Only Johnny Henderson, Charlie Shelp, and myself was left, and I was glad to be with Johnny since he is as near a friend as I have. We was also joined by a new man from Syracuse—Washington Evans.

Washington said his father is a carpenter and that after the war he would be, too, and it turned out to be a great fortune to have him when we built our stockade tent. Ours is sturdier than most, with a tightly constructed stone-and-stick chimney topped by a handsome pork barrel. Inside, Washington put together furniture, including a barrel table and four stools. We are the envy of the Company and even Lt. Toms came out of his tent to inspect our work and said it was the coziest he had ever seen. Eight new men have joined G Company, tho none are as welcome as our Washington.

View of our stockade tent. That is Washington Evans sitting in the doorway talking with Johnny.

Had the shakes for five days, but not bad enough to visit a doctor—thank Heavens! That Reb boy came back a few times in my dreams, but has faded away again. The only thing we lack now is food—or rather a variety of it, corn being plentiful. It is hard to believe how many ways we can cook our corn: We have parched corn, boiled-corn dough mush, corn coffee, and the latest invention to make it go down good is to half-parch it and then grind it coarse—like hominy—and then boil it with a small piece of pork as a season. This last is the best by far.

November 20

Very cold, with our day used up stacking boxes and barrels near the commissary depot. Lt. Toms gave instructions and then stood off by himself. He is about as downhearted as a man can get. Lt. Toms was a schoolteacher in a tiny town near Syracuse before the war, but hoped to have a military career after. Now he is certain he will never be allowed to rise above a lieutenancy and that he will always be given the worst assignments. I think he may be right.

The new men are all sick with bowel complaints, tho none are serious cases so far. The good news today is that the boxes and barrels we wrestled contain soft bread and desiccated vegetables, so we will have something to go with our corn!

Later

Johnny and Charlie Shelp have been at it again, and this time Shelp landed several good punches and Johnny's face is swelling up and raw. I wasn't there or I would have stepped between them to spare Johnny some. By the time I heard about the fight and got to our tent, Sgt. Donoghue was telling Shelp to leave Johnny alone from then on. Shelp did not take the Sgt.'s words well and said this was none of his affair, so Sgt. Donoghue—who is a very big man, but of a calm and peaceful nature— usually—hit Shelp so hard his feet left the ground.

When Shelp recovered enough to sit up, Sgt. Donoghue told him to get his equipment and move to the last tent in our row, which is closest to the swamp and not very well made, either. "You can't order me to move!" Shelp shouted. "Only the Lt. can!" "If you want," Sgt. Donoghue said in a low, menacing way, "I will move you myself with this," and he held a fist in Shelp's face. The Sgt. looked around and said, "Williams and Davis, help this man up and to his new home. Wyatt and Doty, get his things out of here. Have one of the new men move into this tent. And, Shelp, if you bother Pte.

Henderson again, you will answer to me. Now *move*!"

The new man's name is Charlie Buell, so we still have a Charlie among us. He is 30, I would guess, or around there, and he carries himself well, being tall and fit looking, and speaking in a clear, precise voice. Like just about every other man who has the ability, Charles has a mustache, tho his is very neatly trimmed. He said he was a lawyer in his home town of Manlius and joined after helping several escaped slaves get to Canada. He seems a good exchange for Shelp and our winter should be more pleasant for it. Johnny is being treated like a wounded hero for having freed us of the enemy. I certainly think he did.

November 23

Capt. Clapp came this morning, and after a brief visit, Lt. Toms was as happy as he has been in a long time. I was glad to see this change in the Lt., but I knew it meant trouble for me and I was right. There is to be some sort of "surprise action" soon and Capt. Clapp wants G Company to be a part of his command. So I will not have a quiet—and safe—winter after all!!

Lt. Toms called the men together to tell us what he knew, which was not much other than we would leave in a few days and be close to the Mine Run River. "We have a chance to prove ourselves," he told us. "Maybe our only chance. I want this Company to be the best in the 122nd." He even asked about the Company journal, which he has not shown interest in for many days. He glanced through it and seemed pleased, but he did say, "Pease, why are you still going on about your bad luck? Didn't your people teach you any better?" I was going to say, "I was brought up on the Bible, which is full of magic and miracles, and even a story about Jonah and his bad luck with the whale. So why is being cursed so strange?" But I didn't because I didn't want to sound like a blasphemer—and I didn't want to miss supper again! "Well, just keep your head down and do what you have always done, and you will be fine, do you hear?" "Yes, sir," I answered, but I can't say that I was much reassured. His only other comment about the journal was that I should list the new men, but I don't want to use up the space til we see who deserts.

The Lt. then sent Caesar to the sutler for some provisions and we are to have a special meal tonight! I was happy then that I had held my tongue. "A Thanksgiving meal," Lt. Toms told us, "for our deliverance."

November 24

Lt. Toms is quite happy today, but the rest of us are feeling stuffed and sluggish because of our meal—which consisted of real eggs, soft bread, butter that was not more than a week or two old, beef stew with real potatoes, dried peaches, and coffee and sugar. After dinner Lt. Toms brought out eight bottles of whiskey — which must have cost a great deal, since we have not seen this in over two months! — and Sgt. Donoghue gave each of us a share in our coffee. It was a fine feast and enjoyable, tho Shelp seems to have turned his mouth on me, repeating often that he did not want to stand near an unlucky Jonah Boy. We will see where this leads.

Asked Corp. Bell, Jehial Lamphier and the Wyatt boys about their pasts, but no one is in a mood to talk, which is just as well because I am in no mood to write.

November 26

Sgt. Donoghue woke us this morning before sunrise with "Happy Thanksgiving. Prepare to march in twenty minutes," and we did, this time as part of Capt. Clapp's unit.

4 o'clock

Crossed the Rapidan River just above the Mine Run River at ten and was immediately given a Reb salute of flying minié balls. Our Company got sent out, along with K Company, to shoo our Secesh friends away while the army marched on.

The woods and underbrush was something thick, so we did not move in any particular order. Crouching low, we went from tree to tree, trying to avoid the hot metal coming at us while working our way toward the sound and smoke of the firing.

I have to admit to being very nervous as we entered the woods. I even started to have trouble breathing and had to take in little gulps of air, but I kept moving forward by watching the man in front of me — who happened to be Johnny Henderson — and dashed ahead whenever he did. My breathing settled down some and was almost normal when I saw something move out of the corner of my eye.

I was sure I had a Reb located — maybe 400 feet away — and I pointed my musket at the tree near his position. I was holding steady, aiming, finger on the trigger, when I heard the loud crack of a shot out of the many that was crackling around me and then the whooshing sound of the ball coming at me.

I know this does not seem possible, but stranger things have happened in this strange war and I know what I heard, so I ducked — and just then the ball sent my forage cap sailing. I was so startled I just sat there on the ground, staring at my cap with its new ventilation hole thru the band and wondering what that ball would have done to my head if I hadn't moved.

"You O.K.? You O.K.?" Johnny screamed in my ear all excited, and I nodded. "Let's go, then! Come on!" he yelled, pulling me to my feet. "Lt. Toms has ordered a bayonet charge and we are lagging."

Johnny started dragging me along, and I stumbled, then righted myself and began to run on my own, fumbling to put on my bayonet as I did. I hardly had a chance to look where I was going before I plunged through a tangle of leaves and branches and followed the others, who was forty feet in front and plunging through leaves and branches, too. Suddenly I found myself very mad at what had almost happened to my head and I wanted to get the Reb who had fired at me, whoever he might be. Lt. Toms was way out in front, maybe 100 feet from me, his sword raised high in his right hand, and shouting "Come on, boys, come on! This way!" and I thought what a fool he was to be out there like that, all alone, and at the same time my legs began moving faster and I made up the ground between myself and the rest of the Company.

I was just a few steps behind one of the new men, with the rest of the Company spread out on either side. I didn't notice anyone else, but I am sure Willie Dodd was near because Spirit, who hadn't been tied up, was to my left and weaving this way and that way through holes in the underbrush and barking madly.

The Rebs was still firing on us and the hissing of lead was all around. Just then the new man went down in a heap ahead of me. That ball was meant for me, I thought, which made me madder still, and then I realized he had just gotten his bayonet snagged on some vines and tripped over his own clumsy feet. But that didn't make me any less mad at the Rebs. I leaped over the new man and a second later I was right next to the Lt. and heading into the smoke of a recently fired Reb gun.

I saw a shadow move up ahead and thought about stopping to fire, when I remembered those shadows coming at us at Gettysburg and thought better of it. I did not want to cause the Lt. any more trouble. So I ran at it, musket lowered now and my bayonet aimed at its center — its stomach — and let out a howling scream that startled even me. Just then the woods in front of me began to crackle like popping corn tossed into a hot fire and the air around me vibrated and whizzed as the miniés flew over, around, and near me.

I had not one thought in my silly head as I ran at the enemy, except that I was going to get the one who shot at me. I did have this strange feeling at the same moment — just a feeling, not any words — that I needed to protect the Lt. — tho why he would need *me* to protect him I wouldn't know.

The smoke from the volley rolled out to meet me and a thought *did* enter my head then. The thought was—on the other side of that smoke are a whole lot of Rebs with muskets and bayonets waiting for you. But by the time that thought was all strung together I was in the smoke and knew it was too late to do anything else, so I screamed again and lunged forward, bayonet extended.

Which is when Lt. Toms's voice broke through clearly: "Pease, what the Hell are you doing? Get back here!" which was also when I came through the wall of smoke and discovered—well, nothing. The Rebs was gone and the only trace of them was their backs as they skedaddled through the trees.

I guess I should have fired on such easy butternut targets, but I was breathing so hard I probably wouldn't have held my musket too steady. Besides I didn't see the point. We had driven them away from the rest of the army, which is what our orders had been.

Lt. Toms and the other men came up then, and everyone started talking at once—the Lt. wanting to know why I'd charged so far ahead by myself and saying I could have been killed, the others patting me on the back and making all kinds of noise about how I'd driven off General Robert E. Lee's army single-handed, that I was a regular hero and so forth. But the only thing I could say between gasps of breathing was "Where is my cap," which Johnny dashed off to retrieve.

That's when Sgt. Donoghue said, "Look at that," and pointed to my stomach. There was a ragged hole in my uniform. I unbuttoned my shirt and pulled out this journal, which I keep in there whenever we leave camp so I will not lose it and so no one else will steal it. The cover, which is of hard board, had a clean hole in it and the ball itself was lodged inside, having made a journey all the way to the entries about Gettysburg.

"Lord," Johnny exclaimed when he came back and examined the hole in my cap and the ball in the journal, "you are one lucky soldier for sure." But I didn't see it that way. As far as I was concerned, the lead was getting closer and closer and it was only a matter of time before it hit its mark.

Only three wounded in our Company — Corp. J. Bell was shot in the leg and the doctor says the bone is broken; W. Zellers was hit in the shoulder, tho the injury is not bad; and W. Bateman had his left eye nearly poked out by a branch he ran into, but he says he aims with the other so he will be okay. Assorted other bruises and sprains and cuts, all minor.

November 27

After our skirmish yesterday, we marched double time

til we caught up with the rest of the 122nd. Lt. Toms received a personal "Well done" from Capt. Clapp and some other officers after K Company's capt. related what took place in the woods. This cheered all of us who want to see our Lt. Toms restored in rank someday. There was nice words for me, too, but by this time I had found my tongue and said I was just following Lt. Toms's orders and had gotten confused in the smoke, which is true, I think. The boys have been studying the recovered ball very carefully and say it is a lucky charm and that I should keep it in my pocket. I said I did not want anything to do with it because metal attracts more metal, so now the boys are going to pass it around among themselves, each one getting to hold it for a day.

November 28

Woke to heavy rain and grumbling thunder. The 122nd was ordered to join up with Gen. Warren's Second Corps, so we and thousands of other soldiers spent the day clomping thru mud. Everyone fears another "mud march" such as we had last January, but that would not bother me. Mud is a lot safer than fighting. Besides, every time I think about what a fool thing I did in those woods and what could have happened, I become very excited and then, afterwards, I get sleepy and want to find a warm blanket. So I am marching with my eyes half open.

November 30

Yesterday we worked like beavers throwing up protective breastworks and preparing to charge the Rebs. The enemy had a strong position, with swamps and gullies behind and to the sides, so any run at them would have been straight on across a wide-open field 1000 yards long. For some reason I continued to be exhausted and fell asleep often, but at least this prevented me from worrying. Even the occasional shots exchanged did not disturb my rest.

At nightfall the order to charge was revoked and we withdrew. Lt. Toms said it was smart to call off the charge since not enough of us would have been left alive to bury the dead. Henry Wyatt called out, "I would have," because he was the holder that day of Lucky Minié, as the ball is now called. "Just stay clear of Jonah Boy," Shelp said. "He is marked, no doubt about it, and

Sgt. Donoghue said I might sleep the war away if I wasn't careful and so I did this self-portrait.

so is anyone around him." Sgt. Donoghue went to say something to Shelp, but I said not to and that he didn't bother me, which wasn't true, but I did not need Shelp to be even angrier at me than he already seems to be.

We are at the Rapidan River today and will cross tomorrow. Lt. Toms thinks our fighting is finished for the year—finally!—and I, for one, will be happy to be back at Brandy Station and in our safe, warm home.

December 2

Arrived in camp to find our tent filled with six loafers! They left very quickly—at our request and Sgt. Donoghue's urging—but it took my tent-mates and me quite a while to clean the mess they left. These loafers was so lazy as to chop up our bench, barrel table, and stools for firewood! They was from a Maine regiment and we somehow would have expected better of them than we got!

I was so tired, I thought I would fall asleep the minute I pulled the covers over me, but I stayed awake a very long time instead, thinking of this and that, but mostly seeing myself running at the enemy and screaming and seeing muskets flashing in my direction. And the dead Reb boy. He had come back, too. I have been in fighting before, but this is the first time a memory has followed me so long after. Is this another part of my bad luck—to remember?

December 3

We built ourselves a bench and more stools, but barrels are scarce, so we have no table yet. Drilled, helped unload wagons, and cleared a section of brush behind the sutler.

I asked Henry Clements about his life and it was as if the Heavens had opened up and a great rain had begun to fall. He talked and talked and talked—a deluge of words—and told me how his great-great-great-*great*-grandparents had settled in New England and raised seven children. Then he told me what happened to each of these children, and their children and *theirs*! It was like all the begats in the Bible—how Cain begat Enoch, who begat Irad, who begat Me-hu'ja-el and on and on—til my head was spinning. If I have this correct, Henry (ours) was born to Henry (the fourth or fifth Henry Clements to appear) and to Henrietta Clark (who was a second cousin of this Henry and who bore a strong resemblance to some other Henry's mother, which created "talk" in the family, it appears). Any-way, Henry (our Henry's father) ran a dry-goods store and livery service and Henrietta gave piano lessons and played the organ in church. They was fairly well off and well connected and had even tried to keep Henry (ours) from having to go into the war by buying a substitute for him, but Henry (ours) did not think it an honorable thing to do, so he enlisted. Henry said he was given a very good education, and even went away to Harvard College, which is a good thing, I think, just to keep all of his relatives straight in his head. I think I will not add another history to this journal for some time.

Johnny is writing home for some herbs to put in a concoction that will, in his words, "let you sleep like a baby even under the barrels of the big guns." I am almost afraid to say it—since I worry that some of my bad luck might rub off on him—but he is as close to a friend as I have ever had.

December 4

Two from our Company deserted last night, and another would have, but a sentry spotted him and brought him in. One of those who got away was our tent-mate Charles Buell. I guess helping a few Negroes get to Canada is a lot different than getting shot at for them! Several men have the bloody flux and are in the hospital, which was a barn before we got here.

Later

The man caught deserting was sentenced to stand on a platform in the middle of camp for twenty-four hours without coat or hat. After this, he will clean out the horse and mule corrals by himself til Lt. Toms says other-wise. Most of us think this a fine enough punishment because he did not run off during a battle. But others — especially his fellow greenhorns — think he deserves something more severe. It is true that in some brigades he could be tried by court-martial, and sentenced to be shot, but Col. Titus has a more lenient attitude with his men.

Of course, a discussion developed over this — soldiers are always scouting for something to yap about — and this discussion boiled up into a little argument when talk got around to the best reason to fight in this war. Sgt. Donoghue said he was part of the regular military before the war and would be after, and following orders, especially to fight, is how you advance in rank and pay. John Farmer said he was a good Christian and that "the bondage of slavery had to be broken once and for all time." George Chittenden said he was also a good Christian but did not care one bit about the Negroes and that they could all go back to Africa as far as he was concerned. He joined because the rebellious states had committed treason and had to be taught a powerful lesson. Lyman

Swim came because two of his friends did and he did not want to be seen as a coward or a Copperhead.

I was asked why I had put my neck at risk, and when I said, "Because I needed a pair of boots and dinner," everybody laughed. But that is the truth. And when the Sgt. asked why I didn't leave after I had got my feet covered and belly full, I got an even bigger laugh when I answered, "Because the boots fit perfect and the dinner tasted good." Which is also the truth. At the time I signed my papers I had been on my own for three months, and while happy to have freed Uncle and Aunt of my bad luck, I have to admit there was too many quiet, hungry nights.

December 5

Drilled in the morning, chopped wood in the afternoon. Lt. Toms was beaming—that is how the Little Profeser described his smile—as he read the part of the official report saying: "Special note is made of the distinguished actions of Cos. K, Lieut. Wooster, and G, Lieut. Toms, who engaged a superior number of enemy skirmishers threatening our line of march and subsequently drove them off." The Lt. was not made a capt., but this recognition pleased us any-way. Of course, Shelp had to say, "Hey, Jonah Boy, they didn't mention you or your hero's charge," and this bothered me more than it should have because I really did not want to be mentioned. Or did not think I did.

Four more men have come down with the bloody flux, so seven are in the hospital now. We also have two cases of the ague—tho I am not one if you do not count waking in the middle of the night with the cold sweats and troubled thoughts.

December 6

Drilled, chopped, ate, looked at the newspaper, and avoided Shelp. That was my day. And wrote this.

December 7

Same as yesterday, tho we did not drill or chop today. Lt. Toms said I might want to add the names of the six new men still here, so I will:

Pte. Washington Evans 19   Pte. John Robinson 35
Pte. Asa Rich 21   Pte. Otto Parrisen 33
                Pte. Hudson Marsh 22
        and the near deserter, Pte. Theron Chrisler 19

No one will have Chrisler in their tent so he is in

a wedge tent by himself near the swamp. Despite his isolation we know when he is near because of the high stink he trails wherever he goes.

Also, I was appointed temporary corp.—because Corp. Bell has been sent north for his broken leg and Corp. Drake has been added to the numbers in the hospital. I tried to say I did not want to be corp., but Sgt. Donoghue said it was not like an invitation to a dance, but an order, and Sgt. Donoghue can be very convincing. I am not the praying sort—not since leaving Uncle's—but I did pray that Bell's leg and Drake's stomach get better fast so I would not be corp. very long. What happened in the woods was an accident and I do not want others to think it will ever happen again.

December 8

Same as above with chopping, but without drilling, tho I did not get to relax with the other men because I had to carry messages for Lt. Toms and Sgt. Donoghue and fill out the roster. Two of my new duties!! The big excitement was the disbursement of a ration of Army whiskey—four spoonsful each carefully dealt out by Sgt. Donoghue. Now, was that not a big drink! I think the Sgt. got the best of this arrangement, as he had a chance to smell the whiskey before we got it.

Decided to try another history and approached William Kittler. But Kittler said he did not want to talk, and when I said it was an order, he said he had no rec-ollection of his parents or where he was from or even of enlisting. Johnny thinks Kittler may be hiding some kind of sordid past. Kittler is always unusually quiet and often goes off by himself, but he has also been an honest enough soldier to date. Johnny joked that I get a history from Shelp, but I am not that brave yet. So I told Johnny it was his turn instead.

Johnny told me his father died when he was young and that his mother raised him and his three sisters on the family farm. "She would get us up and fed, then go out and plow the field or hire a crew to harvest the crops, and then come back and bake pies for the church dinner and such. She has more energy than all of

This drawing is called "All in a Day's Work."

G Company put together." Johnny intends to take up farming, too, and thinks he will marry a girl he knows in a nearby town when the war ends.

December 9

A quiet Sunday at home. The Christian Commission and a pack of preachers descended on the camp and went to every tent looking for like-thinkers. A meeting was to be held on the drill field, with promise of a "free package of useful articles" for those who attend. Some went along to the meeting, but most stayed inside out of the cold, writing letters, reading, playing cards, smoking, and such. I have noticed that in warm weather when we are fighting, many of the men are pious followers, but during the winter when things are quiet and shooting is rare, few respond to the call—unless offered a package. I thought about going myself—to avoid having to deliver messages and for the package—except that the first thing the preacher who came by did was quote the Bible and this reminded me too much of Uncle. So I stayed in our tent and joined pieces of broken candles together to make one good one. Every so often, when the wind shifted, I could hear the sweet sounds of hymn singing and then I listened to the words very carefully.

Sleep still restless but hope for better tonight.

December 10

Very cold during the night and a young snow fell—very unusual this time of the year according to those who know—which has turned everything white and covered many undesirable flaws in the camp—such as our trench latrine. B and H Companies staged a snowball battle, with B Company taking the part of the Rebs. B Company seemed to be getting a thorough drubbing when one of our boys shouted, "Here comes old J.E.B. Stuart and his boys," and we dashed in, scooping up snow and throwing it just as fast as we could til it was H Company's turn to back up. Other companies joined the fight and even some officers, and pretty soon we had a fine battle going with 600 hundred "soldiers" at least. I took a ball of packed ice in the back of the head, but when I turned I couldn't see who had thrown it. I have my suspicions, however.

December 11

Drilled a little, but not with much enthusiasm. The weather is so cold that our hands are numb and there are many long faces in camp. Johnny put together a fine-smelling stew for the tent, but when I put my spoon in for a taste, the pot fell from the pole and most everything was lost in the fire. There was some grumbling about my heavy-handed spooning, but Johnny said it wasn't my fault. He is a steady friend. Had hardtack and what we could salvage from the fire—which was a few potatoes and gritty chicken—as dinner. Word about my accident spread thru camp quickly, because later when out walking, Shelp said, "Hold on to your cooking pots, boys! G Company's Jonah is coming."

Fewer responded to sick call today, tho several—including Corp. Drake—remain in the hospital and are not better despite repeated doses of quinine.

December 15

Boiled our clothes this day and then assembled a nice stew—which did not fall into the fire! Unlike some tents, we *did* clean our pot before going from one activity to the other. The stew was an interesting mix of real and desiccated vegetables and beans, but would have been better if we had added an onion, in my opinion.

December 16

Lt. Toms read this journal and said, "Good God, Corp., next you'll be putting in recipes for pie!" He then said I did not have to write so much and that when I did it should be something "truly interesting or significant, and generally of a military nature." I guess that means I should not mention the outbreak of lice that has laid siege to two tents and threatens the rest!

December 25

Christmas Day began with the delivery of mail and packages. Johnny received a box filled with newspapers, letters, sweets, and canned food. I think he saw that I was all alone in my bed, so he made me help him open all of the little boxes and tins, so that we could sample the gifts. Then he glanced thru a batch of letters and said, "Jim, this one is for you." At first I thought he was joking and I felt embarrassed that I was the only one in the Company with no family outside, but he saw this and added, "I am not joking, Jim. This letter has your name on it. Here," and he handed it to me. I looked at it and could hardly believe what I saw:

Private James Edmond Pease
Company G, 122nd (Third Onondaga) Regiment
New York Volunteers
Army of the Potomac
Brandy Station, Va.

This was the first letter I had ever received in my

life and I was so stunned I looked at Johnny, then at the letter, then back at Johnny. "Close your mouth and open the letter," he said. "It's from Sarah. I can tell her handwriting any-where."

Sarah is Johnny's sister, who is 14, and her handwriting is so small and so finely drawn that I thought it might break into a hundred pieces if I handled the envelope too roughly. But I did manage to close my mouth and open the letter and read it, too, after which Johnny said, "Well, what does it say?" so I read it to him. It was short and I am not sure Lt. Toms would think it "truly interesting and significant," but I certainly do, so I will copy it here:

Dear Private James Edmond Pease,

Our brother Johnny wrote to us about your courageous actions last month, and about the way you charged ahead of the Company to face the enemy alone. We were all very impressed by this, and moved by your valor and bravery, and I wanted to write to tell you that you are in our prayers and thoughts every day. Mother said that Johnny is certainly lucky to have a companion and friend like you, and I agree with her.

With all sincere wishes for your continued health,
Miss Sarah Rebecca Henderson

Johnny grabbed the letter from my hands and looked at it. "If you write back to her," he said, "she will answer you, and I guarantee she will say much more. She is a chatterbox in person and in letters usually." I will write her back just as soon as I can think of what to say.

Among the articles Johnny got was a bag of sleeping herbs that his grandmother put together. They looked like twigs, roots, and leaves to me, but when I boiled them up, the smell was very sweet. Johnny has no idea what is in it. "She goes thru the woods near her house gathering this and that" was all he could say. It tasted just fine. Not strong or bitter. Right now, I feel very sleepy, but I made myself write this so I would not forget the details. Later, in my bunk, I will read my letter one more time and then pull my blanket around me snug. I must say this is the nicest Christmas that I can remember.

January 1, 1864

The Army welcomed the New Year with a cannon salute and the firing of muskets, accompanied by much singing and a tin or two of whiskey. Before going off to be with the officers, Lt. Toms raised his cup and said, "To the best, the most loyal Company in the Army of the Potomac. May we be the first to enter Richmond!" Sgt.

Donoghue stood then and said, "To you, sir. The best any Company *or* any Army can hope to have!" And we all cheered and drank to this because we all believe it to be true.

I am sleeping much better and have not had a visit from my dead Reb friend in days, thanks to the sleeping herbs.

January 2

Began a letter to Miss Sarah Henderson, but after the "Dear Miss Henderson" I did not know what to say. And this was my third attempt to write her! I am not sure what will interest her. I do not think she wants to hear about chimney fires, freezing nights, or the way the measles have the doctors very busy. I will have to think very carefully on this.

January 14

Lt. Toms had me come to his tent this afternoon with the journal. The only other people there was Sgt. Donoghue and Caesar, who unfolded a map of the region on a small table. "Corp. Pease," the Lt. began, "I want you to take careful notes of what is said here." It seems that come spring there will be a major offensive—which is not a surprise since there is always some sort of big action every spring. There would be two parts to this action. One to draw out Gen. Robert E. Lee's army or some part of it—the next to strike at the left flank of his army and get between it and Richmond.

While Lt. Toms explained this, Caesar showed us the most likely route this force would take. At first I was startled to see him do this and not the Lt., since servants—especially Negro ones—are never allowed to be a part of such conversations. I must have looked odd or some such, because Lt. Toms stopped what he was saying and explained that in the past Caesar had been rented out by his master to work on various plantations near Gordonsville. "He knows the roads better than any regular Army scout, so listen when he says something about the terrain or trails or people." I said, "Yes, sir," tho I still found it strange to follow Caesar's dark finger as it moved about the map.

"We have been selected for a special assignment," the Lt. continued. Sgt. Donoghue let out a little groan. The last time we had been given a "special assignment," we trailed along after the supply train. "Don't worry, Sgt.," the Lt. said. "We will be in the thick of it. Capt. Clapp has told me we will support Maj. Pettit's artillery."

When Lt. Toms said this, he was smiling and so was Sgt. Donoghue and so was Caesar. Maj. Pettit is always in the fiercest part of any battle and he is often referred to — behind his back, of course — as "The Merry Widow Maker," because he will hold his guns in place at any cost and seems to enjoy the added excitement. I did not like the sound of this springtime job, and if I smiled it was probably a thin one.

"Needless to say," Lt. Toms said, "this is to be kept secret. Not a word — not a hint — to anyone, not even to those at home. I want you to know because we will begin training with Maj. Pettit, and the men need to learn their tasks perfectly. Maj. Pettit does not tolerate mistakes. And Corp. Pease." The Lt. turned to face me directly and he looked extremely serious. "Keep that journal on your person at all times. I don't want anyone to know what is going to happen."

"Uh . . . y-y-yes, sir," I said, a bit startled. You see, my mind had wandered a little. Cannons are the prime targets in any battle and I was picturing what it would be like being near them during an all-out shelling. "It will never leave me, sir."

"Good," he said. Then, from the table drawer, he took two small pieces of fabric that turned out to be sgt.'s chevrons and handed them to me. "You will be needing these from now on." I looked at what he placed in the palm of my hand, blinked, and must have looked confused. He broke into another broad smile and said, "Congratulations, Sgt. Pease."

He shook my hand, and so did Sgt. Donoghue and Caesar. "But what about Corp. Drake, sir?" I asked. "He is in line next." "He is also being promoted, but he is still too weak from his illness. Besides, we will need three sgts. when we begin this training." "But there are other men, sir, who are older and deserve to—" But he waved my objections aside and said, "I gave this a lot of thought, Sgt. You are the best man to be third sgt. now. Sgt. Donoghue needs help, especially with the record-keeping chores. He will explain what your new duties will be." "Ah, y-y-yes, sir," I stammered again. "Ah, thank you, sir." "No need to thank me, Sgt. You earned those." He paused here, then added, "But do me a favor, Sgt. No more charging the enemy on your own. You make the rest of us seem like laggards." He and the other men laughed very loudly at his joke, and I did, too. A little. Then Caesar produced a bottle of whiskey and four glasses and we all had a drink.

I was still stunned at my promotion, happy about it and a little scared by the new responsibilities, and occasionally—in my head, not out loud—saying the words "Sgt. James Edmond Pease" to hear how it sounded. Then a troubling thought entered my head.

One important duty of a sgt. is to be the first to stand when a charge is called to urge the rest of the men on. It is a little like wearing a red shirt with a great white X drawn across the chest for all of those Reb sharp-shooters to see.

January 15

Took some good-natured kidding about being made sgt. from the rest of the boys last night, but most seemed happy for me. This morning was my first real test.

I called roll, which was not very hard because I know the men. When I said, "Shelp," he did not answer at all, but stood there in the front row with his arms folded across his chest, acting bored. I called his name again and there was still no answer. Some of the boys giggled, thinking it good sport to play with a new sgt., but the look on Shelp's face said he was not playing.

I tried his name a third time, and got an answer, but from another man who said "Here" in a very high voice. This produced a great roll of laughter from the Company and I felt my face flush red. I was about to shout something at the one who had answered and at Shelp when I remembered Sgt. Donoghue's words: "Don't let them get under your hide. If they see they can upset you, they will never let you alone."

So instead I looked at the roster and said, "Pte. Shelp is not here, I guess, and is absent without permission." Everyone knew what that would mean. Anyone reported absent without permission would be put in the cold stockade for a day or two with little to drink or eat, and might possibly be given an aromatic chore such as the one given Theron Chrisler.

Brower Davis said, "But he is right in front of you. Umm, Sgt."

"I did not hear him answer when I called his name," I said. "So he is not here as far as I am concerned. And I don't want to hear any more comments, either." I went to mark Shelp absent when I heard his voice. "Here," he said in a very sullen way, then added, "Sgt. Jonah Boy."

"You will call me Sgt. Pease, Pte. Or do you want to be on report for that, too?"

There was a low murmur from the Company, I think because they felt I was being too harsh on Shelp for such a little thing. But it was not a little thing — not to me — and I wanted Shelp to know it right off. After a moment of silence, Shelp replied, "No, Sgt. Pease, I don't." His voice did not have a minié ball's weight of respect to it, but I had gotten him to answer, so I went on with roll call. Later I noticed that back in our tent Johnny and Washington was both unusually quiet and uneasy around me, so I was glad when Lt.

Toms told me that there was to be a meeting with Maj. Pettit.

7 o'clock

We spent the day with Maj. Pettit and his aides learning how he wants his batteries supported by soldiers. He had a battery of light artillery—six cannons in all—set out in the drill field fully manned, with K, A, and C Companies in support. Usually this kind of instruction would be carried out by one of Maj. Pettit's aides, but there he was in person with his aides looking on. We stood with them on a nearby hill, so we had a clear view of the men's movements.

"Watch how and where they move," Maj. Pettit instructed us. "In battle, there will be fifty to seventy-five guns under my command, but you will be assigned to support just six. Tell your men to stay low when they are in front of my guns or they will lose their heads. And be quick when you move. My guns fire to a rapid count—sometimes every thirty counts—and if you are not down when the count is ended we will not halt the firing, do you understand?" We did.

He was also very particular that we cover his flanks and rear carefully as it is difficult to move hot guns and he did not want to redirect fire unless it was absolutely necessary. "The Rebels lost more men than they could replace last year, so they will not be making so many costly head-on charges."

"That was some show," Lt. Toms commented afterwards as we went back to our tents. "What did you learn from it?" "To move quickly and without hesitation," Sgt. Donoghue said. "To stay low," I answered. "Very low."

I am going to end this now and write a letter to Miss Sarah Henderson so I can share my good news with someone who does not wear a uniform and who is not angry with me. I have not been very successful in writing her before, but now I have something real to say. And I think I will tell her that I have kept her letter in my vest pocket ever since I received it.

January 22

Things still seem strained with the Company. I asked Sgt. Donoghue about this and he said some are probably angry because they was not made sgt., some probably think I am acting high and mighty when I give an order, and some just don't like anyone who is not a pte. "Don't worry about those people," he told me. "They are not worth a bit of thought. Your real friends will always be there." Sometimes, he added, the men do not know how to act, so they become quiet around anyone who has gotten a promotion. "They need to see how you act with them before they can feel comfortable." So I will try to remain calm and see what happens.

Drilling with the artillery battery has begun and Lt. Toms seemed pleased, so I guess we are doing the job — tho it all looks very confused from where I am. The only unusual incident came when Maj. Pettit reviewed his batteries and support and said, "Lt. Toms, your Company is the shabbiest I have seen in a while." Lt. Toms stood tall and said, "It has never gotten in the way of their fighting, sir." And then he added, "We have not been on the receiving end of such supplies since Gettysburg, sir." "Oh, that," Maj. Pettit said, looking annoyed. He turned to one of his aides and said, "Capt., these men are under our care now. See that they are outfitted properly." The next day, like magic, a supply wagon rolled up to our tents with fresh uniforms and boots. I will be glad to be rid of both my old uniform and hat, as the bullet holes are sore reminders of a close call. Too bad I can't get a new book to replace this one. It has more history about it than I want to recall.

February 2

Decided to begin again with the brief histories, hoping this would put the men at ease. I began with Osgood

Tracy because I knew he had a birthday coming up. Osgood said he was born during a terrible blizzard and that his father, who is a surgeon, delivered him and took care of his mother, who had been in labor a long time. Osgood never went to school, except for a few years early on and a year in medical college, but was taught at home by his father and his mother, who spoke six languages between them, including Greek and Latin. He said that they spoke a different language at every meal and that, as far as he is concerned, chicken tastes best in French. When the call came to enlist, his father signed on as a surgeon and is now the brigade surgeon for the 1st New York light artillery; Osgood left school when he heard about his father's enlistment and signed on himself, but as a regular soldier. Osgood also told me that most of the doctors he has encountered in the army—excepting his father, of course—are not fit to lance a boil, let alone treat someone seriously hurt, and that most men die from the "care" that they get and not their wounds. This is something most soldiers already know and is why we avoid the doctors at all costs. But Osgood said I should write it into our Company history so everyone will know.

February 12

Maj. Pettit has us drilling just about every day, with the cannons often firing blank cartridges and other companies playing the Rebs. Some of our Company are beginning to complain, saying they already know how to fight. But fighting under the barrels of cannons with the deafening noise and blinding smoke is a different sort of fighting. Altho not dangerous in the least while they are firing, I can assure you it is very disagreeable, for the concussion of the air almost crushes a person to the ground. So we needed to be out there to get used to the feeling and learn to hear and obey orders.

I said all this to the men and Shelp had to answer back: "And how did you come to know this and the rest of us not?" I felt instantly annoyed by his words — probably more so than I should have — and I was recalling Sgt. Donoghue's advice not to respond too quickly to a taunt when another man — William Zellers, who was not a grumbler — said, "He has seen as many fights as you, Charlie. And been wounded, too." "And," another pointed out, "he has meetings with the Maj. and Lt." "That don't make him an expert," Shelp said. "I didn't say I was an expert," I said in a matter-of-fact way. "But this isn't charging the enemy head on or sniping at him from behind trees. We need to move around more quickly to protect the guns." "It is all a lot of dancing to me," Shelp said, but he wasn't challenging me directly, I think because most of the men, even the grumblers, knew I was right about this. "Give me a good old fight any-time," Shelp added. I knew that our generals aim to give him his wish, but I could not say so.

Received a second letter from Miss Sarah Henderson!!! In my letter to her I had mentioned my unease at keeping the Company journal and in reply Sarah — for she told me I should call her Sarah — sent a silver coin that her great-grandfather had carried during the War of Independence. He was only fifteen when he joined the state militia and in six years of fighting he never received even a scratch. I am not sure about the value of good-luck charms, but I think I will keep this letter and its coin with the other. That way I will not disappoint Sarah.

February 14

Many of the boys in the Company are rereading letters and heaving deep sighs. I began to write to Sarah, and Johnny saw what I was doing and said, "Sarah will think you are in love with her," but he was laughing, so I know he did not intend it in a mean way. Even so I felt myself blushing and had to play with the fire til this passed.

The day was not so cold, so we all spent time out in the sun. Johnny sat on a log for a long time trying to write a letter to his mother.

Sgt. Drake has returned to the Company, and Miles Gorham will replace him as corp.

February 22

I am not sure what to make of this day. We had been running mock battles all day, with K and E Companies charging from various positions. I was running back and forth between Lt. Toms and our men with orders and changes in orders when a spark from the hot guns must have gotten into a caisson because it suddenly exploded and I was the nearest to it. I pulled up straight—I did not even have enough wits about me to duck down!—and one of the wheels flew by my head not more than two feet away, followed by bits of wood and metal and such. I did kiss the ground about then, helped by a rush of hot air, and received a pelting of dirt, rocks, and other pieces of the caisson.

I glanced up, amazed that I still had my head on my shoulders, and I noticed that a few of the men had paused in what they was doing to look in my direction, but not many, and not any of the men at the guns, which still fired away even tho two of the cannoneers had been hit by parts of the caisson, too. The men still played their parts as if nothing unusual had happened.

"Move, Sgt. Pease. If you are not dead—move!" That was Lt. Toms screaming at me. I jumped up and ran as if the Devil himself was chasing me, and I must have been a sight, because I was covered with debris and spitting out dirt. But the orders was delivered and our Company responded. A few minutes passed during which I contained my curiosity, but eventually I had to glance around. Where there had once been a caisson was now a large hole—big enough to bury a man in!—and not much else. When I looked to where Maj. Pettit was, he was still seated on his horse, observing the action. I would wager any amount that he did not even blink when the caisson went up.

Later, back at camp, I heard Shelp's voice, "I tell you, bad things follow him everywhere." He did not use my name, but I don't think he had to. Johnny said I was certainly the luckiest man in the Army. So there are two views of me. Sgt. Donoghue said I had acted well considering what had happened, and I told him I had just jumped at the sound of Lt. Toms's voice. "That is what any good soldier does. He moves when ordered. That's what the men will do for you, too." I wish I could believe what the Sgt. said, but I am not sure many of the men will ever jump at my voice — or that I will live long enough to give many orders.

The only bright spot is that today I received a third letter from Sarah, and Johnny said, "She is sweet on you, Jim. I can tell." I would write her a letter about my day, but my head hurts painfully, so I will boil up the last of my sleeping herbs and try to rest instead. But I will keep the words "she is sweet on you" in my head.

February 25

Maj. Pettit has us learning how to load, aim, fire, and maneuver the light artillery, as well as all commands. "You should know the procedures," he explained, "so you can fill in when any of my men are wounded or killed." The Little Profeser noted that the use of the word "if" would have suggested that something *might* happen, while the word "when" means it will *certainly* happen. It is sometimes hard for me to recall that I joined this army to get a pair of boots and dinner! Now look where I am! Head no longer hurts, tho I am still wary around the caissons when the guns are hot. A sound sleep is once again hard to find.

Approached Niles Rogers about a brief history, but he said his throat hurt and I should ask his tent-mate Philo Olmstead. Philo grew up in Belvedere, New Jersey, where his father was an undertaker. "One summer we had a fever that carried off a lot of folk and we buried a good part of the town. When the fever passed, the town was mostly young, and then there wasn't much business for my father and we had to leave. So we traveled into New York and didn't stop til we came to a town with a lot of old people. Business has been good ever since!" Despite his background, Philo is a very merry soul and is always ready to laugh. When I asked him why he didn't go into the burying business, he said, "It's usually steady work, but I prefer to deal with my neighbors when they can talk back, so I became a carriage maker."

Sent a brief letter to Sarah telling her about my "near miss." Johnny said he was going to write Sarah and say that I "pined" for her so much that the earth shook and exploded under my feet. I then "ordered" Johnny not to write about the incident—so being a sgt. has some advantages.

March 7

Spring must be near because enemy skirmishers have been hitting and jabbing at us at various places for the past week or so, and we have been doing the same for them. Lt. Toms says that Gen. Lee and the Rebs are probably cooking up their own spring plans and he just hopes we can get ours going before they do theirs. Accompanied Maj. Pettit's guns to meet Rebs wandering nearby, but they skedaddle whenever artillery arrives. The Maj.'s men can unhitch, load, and fire so quickly that most of the time the Rebs are not out of range and it is always a lively sight to see them dance from the shells.

I have been looking for a letter from Sarah these past days now, but there is never mail for me. Has she forgotten me already? I asked Johnny if he had gotten any mail and he said no, but he did say he had "disobeyed orders" and written Sarah about the caisson exploding—he said because he knew I would not say enough about it—tho he swore he did not put in anything about my pining away.

March 11

We have just learned that there is a new commander of the National Army, Lt.-General Ulysses S. Grant. Everyone was happy that Gen. Meade will stay to command the Army of the Potomac, since he is well liked by the boys and officers alike. Sgt. Donoghue said we should stop worrying about Gen. Meade and start worrying about our skins, since a new commander will always try to prove he deserved his promotion with a victory—and guess who will have to do the fighting.

Still no letter.

March 16

It happened very quickly. Yesterday Lt. Toms was called to a meeting and immediately after he issued orders to pull down our winter homes and be ready to march. We are now moving along the pike road at a leisurely pace in the general direction of Jefferson. Winter is over officially, I guess, and now the fun begins. No more time to write.

March 17

Have begun a letter to Sarah, but don't know when I will be able to send it out. We are in a wooded section about three miles from main roads, so little mail comes in or goes out. I will continue writing day after day til I can mail it, which will give me something to do besides worry. One good thing about keeping busy—I am so

William Kittler off by himself as usual. When I showed this to Johnny, he said, "He is a strange one, now isn't he?"

tired at night that I drop off to sleep as if I had not a care in the world.

March 23

We have been skirmishing regularly with the Rebs, tho we have had only one wounded seriously — H. Clements — and the boys seem eager to meet the enemy more. Sgt. Donoghue said, "Even Spirit seems more feisty than usual." So far, the heaviest fighting has been over who should be carrying Lucky Minié, which resulted in a flattened nose and a black eye and some hard feelings. There is now an official list which is kept by Corp. Gorham.

The only other "action" to report was my three

skirmishes with Shelp, all very minor, but still annoying. I took the "high road" in all three by letting pass some remarks that could have gotten him time in the stockade, but this did not seem to lessen his anger with me. When I asked Johnny why he thought Shelp acted this way, Johnny said, "Some people are born mean and that is the way they live and there is no explaining it." I guess that is as good an explanation as any.

March 24

Chased the Rebs most of the day, but to little purpose. Our line of march has been altered and we seem to be heading back toward Brandy Station. Lt. Toms told Sgt. Donoghue, Sgt. Drake, and me that 30,000 troops have left and are headed south. "Let's hope Uncle Robert bites at the apple," he said. "Then we will take a bite out of him."

It has been over a month since I last heard from Sarah. Johnny has received only one letter from his mother and none from his sisters or other relatives in this time, and thinks there is mail for us sitting in a wagon in some farmer's pasture. Sent off my last letter to Sarah and will start another.

March 25

Rested today and so did the Rebs, so it was quiet and peaceful. The rain that has fallen all night and today probably has something to do with this. Have lived on hardtack, salt pork, and corn meal for a week now, so I traded two pounds of tobacca for a chicken—a steep price—and boiled it up in a coffeepot with some root vegetables and salt. Drank the soup from the spout and found it very good, and Johnny agreed.

Some letters and packages caught up with us in the afternoon, but none for me. Three months ago I would not have even given it a thought. Was able to finish my letter to Sarah and mail it out. Once it was gone, I wondered if writing before she has replied to my other letters will offend her as too forward. Johnny said, "At least you're not thinking on being bad luck and such any-more." Which is not true, not exactly any-way, but I did not confess this to Johnny. He then added, "She loves to get letters, especially from you, so don't worry about writing too much."

March 26

Have not moved and all remains quiet and wet. Rumors drift thru camp about what is happening and where we will be headed next and some of the boys even say we are going to try to get between Gen. Lee's army and Richmond—tho I never say yes or no. Pete McQuade asked if I knew something I wasn't telling and when I said no, he became upset, wanting to know why I wouldn't tell him. He says he needs to know if we are going to fight in a day or two days or a week or two weeks, that he feels that something bad will happen to him and he wants to be prepared. It seems that his turn with Lucky Minié was two days ago and will not come up again for nearly a month, so he is nervous. I was not sure what to say or do, and he seemed very serious, so I gave him the silver coin Sarah sent me and told him its story. I hope Sarah will understand why I did this.

Received back pay today!!! Many of the boys have set to gambling it away, but I put my money in a sock and will hold it til I know what to do with it. Johnny said that since our pay is here, our mail will probably follow—on July 4th!

Later

At dinner, Willie Dodd asked that Spirit be given a regular turn with Lucky Minié, saying he was as much a part of G Company as any of the rest, but the boys voted this down. Willie was upset, of course, but he seemed better when I asked him for some history. His mother died when he was just five, and his father was—and still is—an engineer for the New York Central Railroad, so Willie has spent most of his life on trains going from one town to another. He came by Spirit after the dog was hit by a train—not his father's—and lost its front leg. "But don't feel sorry for him," Willie said. "He can outrun most any animal and I can't think of anything he can't do that a dog with four legs can—except lift his leg to pee." Willie was just fourteen when he enlisted, and when I asked how he had managed to pass—him being four years under the legal age to enlist then—he said he guessed he got in on his length. Willie is tall for any age. He said that after the war he intends to join the railroad and maybe be an engineer himself someday, which I think will suit him as he is always on the move whether in camp or not. Willie wanted to know how I had managed to enlist, and I had to admit I had lied my way in. I signed Uncle's full name to the paper saying CONSENT IN CASE OF MINOR, and when questioned about it said, "You can check with him yourself if you don't believe me," but the recruiter only grunted and then went on to the next man in line.

April 2

Broke camp and did more marching. I am not sure how all this helps us to beat the Rebs, but we have seen a great deal of Virginia and its people. Not many are openly hostile toward us, tho a few — mostly the old people — tell us we are trespassers and robbers and Yankee trash. The rest just stare at us when we pass thru a town and keep their thoughts inside — which is wise when there are so many soldiers near who want a fight. The Negroes give us very little response, tho now and then one or another will nod as we go past or tip their hat if no Secesh white man is around to see them. Several have run off from their owners and joined our march as camp servants. So far no Southern owners have come asking after them — and I doubt many will!

April 9

Well, after more marching and no fighting we have settled down in a grassy spot and pitched our tents. We have been put in reserve and Lt. Toms said, "Enjoy this while you can." The newspapers are full of stories about the action south of here and "hints" of what might follow. These hints sound as if the writers were in the tent with Lt. Toms and the rest of us last January! I wonder if Uncle Robert reads the same newspapers as we do!!!

Later

Mail has arrived—with three letters for me!!! Johnny saw me reading them and said, "I think I will have a sgt. for a brother-in-law any day now!" I took a good deal of ribbing from the other men after this but managed to give some of it back, as almost everyone has letters today.

April 12

This spot filled up pretty fast and soldiers are now camped in a farmer's field and orchard. Most are Gen. Warren's men—our own 122nd is not in sight—and more are expected every day. A long line of wagons went by today and we even saw some familiar faces among the mules and drivers.

The only thing of note today is that I had another skirmish with Shelp. He and some other men were playing cards when a dispute broke out and Theron Chrisler called Shelp a cheat and Shelp called Theron a whiny coward and threw over the table to get at him. I got between them and some other men grabbed hold of Shelp—which was lucky for me because I think he would have hit me just as well as Theron. I told Theron that he had better have proof of what he said and when it was clear he had none—other than that Shelp had won about all of his money! — I told him that I had never known Shelp to cheat and that if he didn't watch out — but I never got to finish because Shelp started yelling, "I don't need your help! I can take care of him!" And he tried to get at Theron again, but the men held him back. I ordered the men holding Shelp to take him off somewhere to settle down and he went off with some very hot words for Theron and me! Next, I told Theron that I did not want to see him gambling again — ever — since he did not know how to lose and that he should get to his tent fast before I got angry. I have a feeling that I will hear from Shelp again, even tho I did stick up for him.

April 22

Have not had time to write in this journal what with filling out the roster reports for the paymaster and other sgt. chores. I have only found time to write Sarah two very brief letters since her three arrived, but I will try tonight after final roll call. I asked Johnny if Sarah's hair was a little or a lot curly and he responded by telling me he was tired of telling me this detail and that about her and having to tell her this detail and that about me. "Go get your picture taken and have her send you one of her and be done with it!" I think this is a very good idea.

April 24

Went to town to have a picture taken but no one there has a camera—or if they do they don't want to take a picture of a Yankee. Sgt. Donoghue said there is a newspaper photographer somewhere in camp and he might take my photograph, so I am going out now to find him.

Later

I hunted and hunted all over the camp, but it is not easy to find one man among 3000! Finally I came on Mr. Thom. Roche and his photographic wagon and he made a carte-de-visite photograph of me in my uniform for one dollar. I thought the price a little steep—especially since it did not take more than a few moments to take the picture—but Mr. Roche said that chemicals are dear down here, especially since every officer in camp wants to sit for a picture. Now to finish my letter and send it—and me—off. I wonder what Sarah will think.

April 30

Lt. Toms said to be ready to move in the morning. I guess our little rest is at an end.

May 2

We have been marching, sometimes double time. Covered fifteen miles yesterday despite poor roads and heat, leaving behind extra clothes, books and whatever else was not absolutely necessary. Lt. Toms did not say much to me all day other than "Keep them moving, Sgt. If the Maj. can keep his guns moving, we can keep our men moving." At one river crossing, one man — George Chittenden — was swept down water, but we managed to drag him to shore before he went under. We heard later that two men was not so lucky when their wagon overturned.

George Chittenden drying his shoes after his morning swim.

Today we covered eighteen hard miles and the men are exhausted. Several of them are missing tonight due to straggling. Sgt. Donoghue is doing paperwork and Sgt. Drake is no-where to be found, so I am going back for the missing men on my own.

Later

Went back a mile or two and found four of our men off to the side of the road in a cozy glen with men from other companies who had also dropped out of the line of march. There was a fire and a pot of coffee and a kettle with some sort of bean stew boiling away—a pleasant domestic scene, I thought.

When I entered, most of our men seemed embarrassed—at not having kept up with the rest of the Company and at having been sought out like schoolchildren—but they was nice enough and even offered me a cup of coffee. Charlie Shelp was there and was not happy to see me.

I told our men that Lt. Toms wanted them back in camp and Shelp said, "I am not leaving til I eat." The men not from G Company encouraged Shelp, and one said, "You can't order an injured man to march and this man is injured. I saw him limping myself. It's against the rules." Shelp looked pleased that he had such loyal supporters and shook his head in agreement. I may be mistaken, but I believe Shelp's courage was bolstered some by the whiskey the men was passing around. "Yes, it's against the rules," he agreed.

If I was Sgt. Donoghue, I would have made Shelp and the others obey with my fists, but I am a full head shorter than the Sgt. and a lot lighter. There was not much I had to use against them except my words, and I wasn't sure they would work. "If you are really injured," I said to Shelp, "you should report to the doctors. But you don't look injured to me, Pte., just hungry. Have your dinner and then find us up the road a ways."

The men from our Company seemed happy with this solution and even some of the other men—the ones who had backed Shelp—looked satisfied. But Shelp said, "You can't make me go to the doctors. You can't make me do any-thing!"

"I am not going to make you do any-thing, Pte. But I will tell you that when final roll call is taken tonight, you had better be in camp or at the doctors and not in between."

Shelp began to say more, but I turned from him, wished the rest of the men a fine meal and said good night. Sgt. Donoghue would have had those men marching back with him and no back talk either, so I felt very much alone as I walked to where we had camped. I am not at all sure I am up to this business of being a sgt.

10 o'clock

Final roll call taken. All but C. Shelp are in camp.

May 3

Shelp still absent, and the assistant surgeon in charge of the field hospital says no Charlie Shelp is in their care.

85

We are to march at any moment, so there is no time to look for him, or to write about it.

May 4

We have met up with the rest of the 122nd—and the rest of the Army as well!—and crossed the Rapidan at Germanna Ford. We was near the head of the march and among the first across with orders to go up the Culpepper Plank Road a mile and hold the area til the rest of the army could get across. A force of Sheridan's cavalry has already swept ahead to clear the roads, and we are to follow them as closely as possible to rid the surrounding woods of Reb skirmishers.

The land is fairly open and rolling here, with stands of trees and some burned-out houses about, but mostly unplowed fields. A dark line of the woods is up ahead to greet us and is why the area beyond is referred to as the Old Wilderness on most maps. Lt. Toms said that we might have 80,000 to 100,000 troops behind us by tomorrow night.

Noon

We was ordered forward again and told to secure another mile of the road. There are about 400 soldiers in this group, plus a number of Maj. Pettit's light artillery and some cavalry. Behind us we can see the landscape already swarming with troops and wagons and ambulances and other equipment. I am not happy to be showing myself so clearly to the Rebs, but I must admit to a proud feeling when I see so many fellow soldiers.

We had just begun to move when Charlie Shelp suddenly appeared, panting heavily and covered with leaves and dirt and looking as if he hadn't slept a wink. The others greeted him warmly and he was smiling when he joined the march, and I might have let him alone and been done with it, but I couldn't. If I didn't say something to him, then I would not be doing my job and who knows what he or someone else would do next. So I called out, "Pte. Shelp, you will step out of the line."

I admit that I was about as scared as when we go into a fight, but I went over to where he was by the side of the road any-way. "You did not report for roll call last night or this morning. Do you have a reason for being absent?" "I was at the doctors," he said, "having my injury treated." "Then you have your discharge orders from the doctor," I said. He looked startled for a second, then felt his vest pockets and said, "I guess I dropped them. When I was running to get back here." "You weren't with the doctors, Pte. I checked. You are on report, and when we are finished out here, you will be dealt with, do you understand? Now get back in line." Shelp stood quiet for a few seconds and I could tell he wanted to hit me, only too many was around to see and his punishment would be even more severe if he did that. But as he walked past me he mumbled, "We will see who gets back, Sgt."

If I was scared before, now I was stunned. A few moments ago, I had to worry about the enemy I might have to face. Now I have to worry about the one who is marching along with me as well.

6 o'clock

At around 2 o'clock the woods closed in on both sides of the road, a scraggly collection of oak and pine trees — alive and dead, standing up and falling over — with vines and ill-formed shrubs all around. The road is about twenty or thirty feet wide, so we had to march shoulder to shoulder, and what a tight feeling that gave us all.

A little on and we halted and sat by the side of the road, having a hardtack "meal." The officers had a meeting and then we sgts. met with our lts. — and they told us to be alert and that we might run into the enemy at any moment. Both things we all already knew, but the officers, being mostly lawyers, probably thought it best to hand down this "information" officially.

When I got back to the men, I found Johnny writing to his mother and sisters. I told myself that I should write Sarah just as soon as my sgt. duties allow, which might be a while. I noticed how steady Johnny's hand was and commented on how calm he seemed. He said he is all excited inside but does not see the point of showing it. "I will either survive a fight or not and it isn't in my hands any-way," he said, and looked up. "He knows what will happen to me and that is good enough for me."

Most of the men believe similarly, while a few believe there is no Divine hand involved in any of this. When I was with Uncle and Aunt, they said God rewarded us according to our thoughts and deeds. I can understand that I have been bad enough to wind up here, but I cannot believe that Johnny has done anything to deserve being shot at or killed! And if he hasn't, then why is he here? I am not smart enough to see what the grand scheme is, but these thoughts rattle around in my head and I try to make some sense of them.

The bugle has sounded and we are about to march on. I glanced up and saw our men getting ready to march. Then I spotted Shelp. He is on the other side of the road staring right at me now—right through me!—his eyes as dark and as menacing as any stormy night. I am telling myself to be calm and finish up this entry, but a cold shiver goes thru me any-way.

9 o'clock

After our stop we went another mile more along the plank road, then took a smaller road—more like a rough path—that went off to the right into the thickest sort of woods imaginable. This path is not much wider than a wagon and in bad condition with no bridges over streams, so our progress has been slow. We have stopped so the officers can talk over the latest scouting reports.

Lt. Toms told Sgt. Donoghue, Sgt. Drake, and me that Lee's army is five or ten miles from here and headed our way. Fast, according to the scouts. "They aim to catch us in these woods," the Lt. said, "so we can't maneuver and use our numbers to full advantage. I don't think they'll do anything tonight, but we have to get the men ready for a real fight." So I guess Uncle Robert was not fooled a bit by the first soldiers that went out.

We are to move ahead another half mile or so, then put up breastworks for tomorrow's fight. The only other thing we know for sure is that we will be on the extreme right flank of our line of battle.

May 5

This is the wildest mess of woods I have ever been in and believe it is correctly named the Old Wilderness. We happen to be near a substantial clearing in the woods—a very rare thing as far as I can tell—with our cannons on a slight rise with a good view to the other side. Maj. Pettit has left twenty cannons here at the clearing, back a little in the woods and concealed by leaves, so they are not easily seen.

This open section appears to have been an expanse of swamp or bog that dried up years ago and left a scattering of dead and collapsed trees, a shaggy grass covering, and some exposed boulders and rocks. The Lt. told us that our line of battle runs for almost two miles to our left, in the general direction of Spotsylvania Court House, tho the trees and shrubs are so thick that you can't tell if a line exists. The rest of Maj. Pettit's guns are scattered along this line, and he is as agitated as a thunderstorm because the trees will make it hard to use his artillery to best effect any-where but in the few open sections. We have been listening to the sound of heavy fighting since the sun came up, so the cannons have not been totally silenced.

It is quiet here—or I would not be writing this!—and we feel quite isolated, but this has given the men a chance to make coffee and breakfast, and speculate on what might be going on.

I have the new men to watch over, including Theron Chrisler. Also Johnny Henderson, Boswell Grant, Niles Rogers, and Willie Dodd are with me, and of course, Spirit is, too. Sgt. Donoghue said to keep a sharp eye on

Chrisler, and to shoot him—in the back, if need be!—if
he tries to run off again. I am not sure I will do this,
since I share his fear, if not his inclination to run. That
is my group and I am happy with them—and happy that
I do not have Shelp to deal with.

Our job is very simple. Last night we took down a
line of trees to one side of the clearing for some 300 feet
and removed brush in front as best as possible. Now my
men are positioned every twenty or thirty feet along this
rough breastwork. Out in front of us are C, A, and K

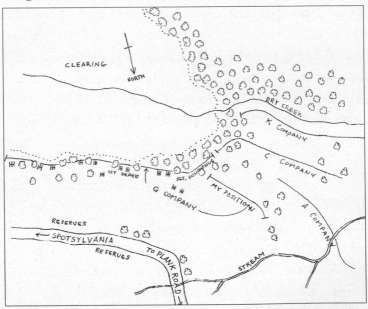

*Johnny thinks this map is accurate, but he says my trees look like heads of
broccoli. I would "plant" even more — since the woods are very thick in
here — but my hand is tired.*

Companies. If the enemy tries to get around our flank, they will hold them back out there. If they can't, we are back here to give them covering fire til they reach us. Maj. Pettit sent word that we are not to surrender this spot *on any account*, so this could become a very hot place if the men out in front can't hold them. There are more reserves behind us on the path in case they are needed along the line of battle, and I think there are other companies out in the woods, but who can tell?

Later

We was just beginning to enjoy a restful morning when the first Rebs struck, at around 11 o'clock. The fighting from earlier seemed to be coming down along the line of battle, getting closer and closer, but very slowly so it was not at all alarming. We heard bugles and the report of a cannon from the other side of the clearing after 10 o'clock, but then the sound died away and we settled back again, supposing that they had decided to make a fight somewhere else. Some men even began making plans for dinner!

Sgt. Drake thinks it was a trick of the wind, that the fighting was actually close by, but the sounds got lost in the woods and did not reach us. Whatever the truth, suddenly our advance pickets began speaking in the woods across the way, which was followed by a stern volley from the enemy. Then our pickets came across the clearing on the double-quick, calling that the Rebs was on their heels—which any fool with ears and a brain already knew.

. I did not have the best view of any of this, being 200 feet from the closest gun with my back to the clearing, tho I turned often to see what was happening. I was watching when our pickets reached the breastworks and threw themselves over. A scattering of Rebs had entered the clearing by this time, some firing our way, others kneeling to reload, the rest coming on. Around this time, Maj. Pettit nodded to one of his aides, who gave the order and one cannon fired canister at the enemy—which sent a hail of metal pieces into the faces of the closest Rebs. This seemed to cool the fighting spirit of them all because they stopped what they was doing and dove for the ground—and I would have done the exact same!—and the attack ceased right there. Maj. Pettit did not have his other guns fire at the enemy as they dashed back into the woods, which seemed odd, but at least the few Rebs we saw are gone.

Fighting continues in the distance to our left—tho few messages have been received today and the path behind us is still jammed with soldiers, so there is little traffic along it. We may be so far out here that no one cares about us or this patch of dirt. Let's hope so.

In the evening

They came on at dusk—something Lt. Toms suggested they might do. So I guess they care. The shadows was beginning to lengthen when first one Reb soldier, then two, three, four, and more scurried from the far woods, bent low and searching for what little cover there was. These advance pickets had been sent out to see what we would do.

Naturally, our men opened fire on the shadowy targets and may have picked off one or two. It was hard to tell. Ten more entered the clearing in the meantime, moved forward 100 feet, dodging and ducking, and went to ground when they found shelter. Pretty soon this small group had miniés whistling thru the spring leaves at us and it was our turn to duck.

"Find your targets before you shoot," I heard Sgt. Donoghue order, as he moved among his group. "Make your shots count. Don't waste a single shot." Which was good advice, so I went along my little line and told the same to my ten men. We had been issued sixty rounds yesterday, but getting resupplied in this tangle of trees will be hard. Our sixty shots might have to last all night and tomorrow.

Sgt. Donoghue appeared at my side. "Listen for our pickets out there," he instructed me, tho he really didn't need to. I had no intention of being caught "napping" and then have to answer later to him, Lt. Toms and Maj. Pettit! He had just finished speaking when—*whiz! bang!!*—a shell burst over our heads and—*fiz! whiz!! rattle!!!*—the fragments came tearing thru the treetops above us, which made us duck even lower and grab hold of our forage caps. When the metal stopped falling, the Sgt. looked up at the leaves above, which had been clearly punctured in many places by the metal, smiled and said, "I guess it wasn't our time. Good luck, Pease," then hurried off.

We went back to our work then, which became real when the advance pickets from K Company began to be heard. My breathing got faster and I had an odd sense that things was beginning to happen too quickly around me to see.

There are two kinds of charges that I know of. In one, everybody jumps up right away and runs at you, that is, after the cannons have softened up the other side. This is the sort of charge that the Reb Gen. Pickett made at Gettysburg. The second begins slowly, with little groups of men moving forward, poking and probing in various places to find the softest spot to charge. So in a little while, if they think ours is the easiest to get thru, the charge will come—and it was this that had me edgy.

"Steady! Steady!" I yelled at my group, but I was really yelling at myself not to think too much. If you don't do much thinking, but watch instead and then let your feet and body react, you can keep the creeping shakes under control. "Keep those fingers off the trigger," I added, just in case any of the new boys was feeling as jumpy as me and might twitch their trigger finger by accident.

All around us it seemed that muskets was barking and chattering away, punctuated every so often by the sound of a cannon and the *whooosh* of a shell overhead followed by its explosion — tho we still couldn't see what was happening.

"Look, Sgt.," Boswell — who was closest to me — shouted, pointing to the clearing. I glanced around and saw a line of butternut uniforms break from cover and begin running across that open space toward our line. Then I heard the sound — a steady wave of it, like the scream of 1000 wounded animals gone crazy with pain. I'd heard it before, but every time they let out their Reb Yell, I have to admit it chills me to the bone. Every so often one of these charging men would be hit by a bullet and fall, opening a gap in their line. Pretty soon this first line looked like a mouth of rotten teeth — tho none of those still running seemed inclined to turn back!

When the first group had come about 100 feet, their advance pickets stood and joined the charge, while behind them a second line of men emerged from the woods. They was shoulder to shoulder, almost touching each other they was so close, and screaming as loud as the first line. Thinking back, I guess that somewhere between 300 or 400 men was charging toward our guns, maybe more.

That is when I realized what had happened. Earlier, Maj. Pettit had fired only one gun, which was enough to warn off the enemy. But they was back now and eager to get that gun — not realizing that a lot of others waited also. The Rebs was about halfway across when the trap — for that was what it was — was sprung and the entire battery fired with an unholy explosion that made the ground and trees quiver. A wall of smoke was instantly created, making seeing even worse, but I saw enough to know that the metal pieces ran across the clearing like a hot scythe, cutting down men, grass, and any-thing else standing.

The damage to the enemy line was severe and their screams terrible, but it did not stop their charge or our work. I turned my attention to the woods down in front of us, where the fighting was getting louder, and I noticed that some of A Company's men was moving forward. I shouted to my group to be alert and to stop watching the clearing.

Another volley from our cannons erupted, followed by more screams and the rapid *snap-crackle* of both sides' muskets. The breeze shifted, pushing smoke over us and filling up the woods around us. It had already gotten pretty dim, but now the smoke made seeing impossible. In front of us smoke and shadows and more smoke and shadows drifted thru, with an occasional flash of yellow-blue to indicate the position of a musket. I was already nervous enough, but not being able to see made my stomach jump. That's when I decided to make some quick visits — as much to distract myself as to make sure my men was okay.

Boswell was first and I told him to watch the clearing and shout if anything happened there. Then I hurried on. Not much fire was being directed at my group, but miniés sailed over our heads any-way, so I was bent over low when I ran to the next man. That was Theron Chisler, and he was peering ahead so intently that he jumped a little when I threw myself down beside him. "You O.K., Theron?" I asked, and he nodded yes. His eyes was big and round and I thought I should say something to put him at ease. "Good," I said, and added, "but I can tell you that I wish those fellows would go home for the night so I can get something to eat." Theron cracked a smile and said he agreed. Then I told him, "Stay low, hear? I'm going to check on the others now. And don't shoot unless you know what you're shooting at, okay?" He nodded again, and then I moved on, going from man to man, and saying much the same to each.

When I got to Johnny, he seemed very snug and not at all concerned. He was at a spot where three trees had come down, and he had piled up bits of wood and rocks to either side of his position so he could see thru a tiny slit between the trees. If an enemy minié ball was looking for him, it would have to have very sharp eyes. The last one on my line was Willie Dodd, who was tucked in behind a thick section of tree trunk and happily feeding Spirit hardtack. "Evening, Sgt.," he said as if nothing unusual was happening around him. "Care for dinner?" I patted Spirit and took a cracker, only when I bit into it my mouth was so dry it just sat in there like chalk.

I looked around quickly, making a real show of studying what was going on in front of us, but of course, I couldn't see any-thing at all. There was shadows moving around out there, but nothing that suggested the Rebs had broken thru, no shouted warnings or urgent bugle notes. The heaviest fighting was still coming from the clearing, which was now way off to my left. Just then, our cannons roared again and I pulled my head back behind the tree and gulped that wad of dry hardtack down, but it got stuck in my throat.

"That was something, wasn't it, Sgt.?" Willie said.

I nodded, forcing the hardtack the rest of the way down, then managed to say, "Almighty fierce. Sounds like Maj. Pettit has added some guns over there."

A moment later, a cheer rose from those very guns and told us the Rebs had given up the charge across the clearing and was withdrawing. The firing continued for fifteen or twenty minutes, then died away very quickly. There was a series of shouted commands—to stop shooting, to move this company or that one here or there, to see who had been wounded—and then things quieted down. The only sounds left now was the moans and cries of the wounded, most of whom was lying in the clearing.

I went back along my line and did another check of my men. A number of men from K and one or two or three from A and C Companies were being helped to the path where they would wait for the ambulances, but I think it safe to say that we did not suffer many losses or serious injuries tonight. Lt. Toms said the Rebs was "stubborn in their fight, but not dogged"—which may mean that we are not very important to their plans. Time will tell.

Sgt. Donoghue came over to see how we had done and said that no one from our Company had been killed, tho three had been hit by exploding shells: T. Stevens, D. Bernard, and C. Mahar. Fighting up the line had sounded very heavy—heavy enough to have most of the reserves on the path behind us moved up the line away from us—but there is no way to tell what has happened.

10 o'clock

When things settled down, a flag of truce appeared from across the clearing and after some talk the Rebs came out to collect their dead and wounded. The wounded was easy to locate because of their moans and cries for help and water, but it took some time to find all the dead. Ten or more men with torches roamed here and there to search in every dark spot. I remembered the dead Reb boy we'd seen in the woods and thought it a shame that he hadn't been found like these fellows here.

Some friendly chatter was exchanged with the searchers and one Reb—who was forty feet from our breastwork—said, "See you in the morning, Yanks." But he made a mistake in addressing his comments near Shelp, who responded, "We will see you dead and in Hell, Johnny." I believe that Reb was genuinely surprised by Shelp's tone and thought him rude—and so did I.

I have to do a report on my men and then Sgt. Donoghue, Sgt. Drake, and I are to meet with Lt. Toms. I am going to write a quick letter to Sarah and have decided to send all of my money to her for safekeeping. Later, I will get someone heading to the rear to take my letter back. This will take most of the night but I am glad for the distractions.

May 6

Did my report, had my meeting, wrote my letter, and even found someone to take my letter out—for $1!—and then had to stand guard between 2 and 3 o'clock A.M. Nothing unusual moving "out there" except a thick, damp fog. After this, managed to close my eyes—for ten minutes, I think!—and then it was 5 o'clock and time to get up and get ready to greet the Rebs.

K Company—who felt the hardest fighting yesterday—was replaced by reserves. C and A Companies both asked to be left in place, and three other companies was moved up to add to their numbers. There are now over 200 blue uniforms positioned down in front of me and many more around the clearing. There is a feeling among the officers that they might try to get around us here and then move up our line of battle along the narrow path.

Maj. Pettit relocated his guns—which was hard work in the tangled undergrowth—and four now stand near the middle of my little line.

Had breakfast this morning to the sound of distant fighting. Fog has lifted some and the Lt. said it will burn off by eight, but that we should keep the men alert since our "friends over there" might like to fight with it as cover. I know something is going to happen because couriers have been flying up and down the path since

One of Maj. Pettit's aides scouting Reb positions. Johnny said I was getting better at drawing trees.

5:30 A.M., and the officers have had many meetings.

Someone also thought it important that we receive a supply of ammunition—but no food, so we have only one day's rations left. Pete McQuade joked that the gens. probably don't think many of us will be needing to eat if the Reb forces are as persistent today as they was yesterday. McQuade patted the shirt pocket that held the coin I'd given him and added, "But I'm not worried. Not a bit." This prompted a review of the Lucky Minié list and it turns out that Willie Dodd is to have it today.

Have visited my men many times already. Johnny is in very good spirits despite not having Lucky Minié. He has made his position even snugger with additional piles of wood, and when I greeted him, he asked me how I liked "Fort Henderson." I told him then that I had sent my money to Sarah for safekeeping and he said, "That is almost like a marriage propos

dark it is dark. what time is it? no strength

will try to write—but it is still dark and tired Head
hurts and hurts and tired where are my men and the
sgt., and Lt.?
can hardly see beyond this tree with the dark or is it my
eyes? Voices talking—heard barking—will check. Can
feel pencil—can feel myself writing—must be alive.
Voices all around

Dark still. and head is throbbing still knock I took not
so serious, but every thing is spinning—
Must find a safe place away from here—Rebs
moving everywhere. A voice is talking over and over in
my head—"The way of the wicked is like deep darkness;
they do not know over what they stumble." Familiar
voice—Uncle's? who is the wicked? Foolish to be
huddled here and writing. where are the others?

Later

Sun is just up and I have stopped to rest my leg—
suppose it is may 7 or maybe May 8. I could have lost a
day, I guess. Can see the woods better, but this doesn't
tell me where I am.

Head still hurts, there is a dull pounding behind my left eye and the rest of my body is sore, especially my left shoulder and wrist. Hand numb but nothing broken that I can tell so I count myself lucky—a funny word for me to use— Someone coming

Another Reb patrol. Squads of cavalry and companies have been going by since my eyes first opened after the explosion. Fighting far off, tho where is hard to tell. I don't even know where I am exactly—maybe a mile from where the fight was. Uncle's voice still making visits! No food and need to close my eyes again—will write more later.

Somewhere sometime later

I have found a hollowed-out hole in the side of a hill with shrubs and saplings all around—a good snug place to fit my body. This seems a quiet enough spot, but the Rebs have men roaming about looking for us, so no place is safe for long. Will write what I can remember about yesterday's battle and then sleep. Must travel at night.

Here is what I remember—but I may not recall it all. I was writing in this journal when a bugle sounded and someone off in the woods to my left yelled, "Here they come! Here they come!" Lt. Toms and the other officers was instantly alert and issuing orders; men started running here and there and a scattering of musket fire erupted. The cannoneers all leaped into position, officers ready. Not more than a few moments had passed and the fight was in full swing.

I tucked the journal in my shirt, took up my musket — which I had loaded with dry powder earlier — and turned, ready to fire, when there was a succession of booms from across the way, answered immediately by a full volley from our cannons. Just the thought of the sound made by all the cannons and the way the earth shook makes my head throb even now!

A second later, the ground all around began to erupt as shells hit and exploded and dirt and debris began flying. A shell ripped into the breastworks and instantly killed Niles Rogers and injured Otto Parrisen. Good soldiers both. Another of my charges — Hudson Marsh — cried out, "I am killed, I am killed," and I went over and saw that he had been hit in the shoulder and was bleeding some. "You're not dead yet," I yelled in his ear. "Get yourself back to the ambulances if you have to," but then he realized there was so much metal flying that it was safer to stay put.

I wish my head was clearer. Even now, sitting here in my quiet nest, what happened is still murky. I know our cannons was firing as quickly as they could be loaded, so the ground was in constant motion and dust was jumping up with one and then another and another *Boom!!!* I heard Sgt. Donoghue and Sgt. Drake shouting orders and so I did the same, tho what I said is lost to me.

A shell hit one of the cannons on my line and pieces of it—and the men around it—went flying. I remember thinking, "They have our range now," and seeing Lt. Toms moving among the men, his right arm dangling as if he'd been hit, with Caesar at his side holding him up. I saw men from C Company rushing forward, then almost immediately they was running back, along with some from A Company. A wagon rumbling toward the cannons with fresh ammunition hit the side of a tree and flipped onto its side. I heard 100 shouted orders and the screams of the wounded, ours and theirs—I yelled to my group to be ready to cover our retreating soldiers—there was the sharp blasts of bugle commands and the guns, of course, big and small, popping and booming everywhere. I was disoriented and confused—

Must stop for a moment—to rest and let my thoughts calm down. Can't remember what happened next anyway. The voice—Uncle's I'm sure—is back—"The shield of his mighty men is red, his soldiers are clothed in scarlet. The chariots flash like flame when mustered in array; the chargers prance." How many times did I copy these lines? How many times did Uncle read and mark my mistakes and make me copy them again?

Later

I was sleeping peacefully with no dreams in my head at all when suddenly I heard a voice shouting in my ear—a new voice—Corp. Gorham's. I woke up and blinked, looking around quickly to see what the Corp. wanted. But I was alone, of course, and still in my hole in the side of the hill. It is too light to travel, so I will write instead. The Corp.'s voice has helped me remember more.

The battle was going on all around and I was confused when suddenly Gorham was next to me yelling: "Sgt., the Lt. has been taken away injured and Sgt. Donoghue is hit, too. He said to get you."

I didn't respond to him at all. Instead, I looked to see if we had any reserves on the path to help out, but there was none. Then I counted my men to see how many of them was still there. Aside from Parrisen and Marsh, everyone was okay. "Sgt.," Corp. Gorham said, and that brought me back full to the situation.

"I'm leaving you here in charge of these men, Corp. Tell them to stay low and give our men out there good cover," I said, and then asked, "Where is Sgt. Drake? Is he O.K.?" "He is up the line and was fine when I left."

"Good," I answered—because Sgt. Drake was second sgt. and would take over for Sgt. Donoghue. I went to the clearing.

Here it was a mess—blasted holes in the breastworks, our dead and wounded, pieces of artillery here and there, shouting and cries of pain. Shelp was standing up, screaming at the top of his lungs, challenging the Rebs to come and get him and cussing at them. The rest of our men was shooting and reloading as quickly as they could and looking very grim.

Sgt. Donoghue was sitting with his back against the breastworks, shot thru the bowels, holding his guts in his hands and bleeding badly. "Pease," he said clearly, but weakly, "they are going to get thru unless we get help. Keep them . . . the men . . . keep them together. Pull them in . . . close to the guns, hear? Drake is . . ." He winced and looked down at his wound, then looked up at me with an odd little smile on his face. "Doesn't hurt but a little. Strange. Very strange." He was already pale from lost blood, so I told him I would take care of everything and then tried to convince him to go back to the ambulances, but he said no. "Do your work, Pease. Just do your work. Don't worry . . . about me. I will be fine."

I didn't have any idea what to do next, but I thought it couldn't hurt to order Shelp to get down and shoot at the Rebs. "You haven't killed one with your cussing,

Charlie." He looked at me with about the same amount of hate he did the Rebs, growled something at me, but then he ducked down and started shooting. I ran past Shelp and up the line, looking for Sgt. Drake to tell him what had happened to Sgt. Donoghue and Lt. Toms and to see if he had any other instructions for me. I probably should have sent another man and gone back to my position, but I was nervous about doing something wrong while waiting for an answer.

I tossed my musket aside as too heavy, so there I was a perfect running target for the Rebs and that thought made me pick up my feet even quicker, I think. Another of our cannons was destroyed and Maj. Pettit's horse was hit. It went down on its front knees and the Maj. had to leap clear before it rolled over on him.

"They are thru on the left!" I heard someone shout from up ahead of me. If that was true, it meant that we was cut off from the rest of the army and any possible help. We was an island surrounded by waves of angry butternut.

I found Drake, who was already responding to Maj. Pettit's orders to relocate his guns. I relayed my information, but all I recall him saying was "Good luck, Sgt. And watch yourself."

The Rebs was coming across the clearing, but their charge was irregular. Beyond Sgt. Drake's position they had gotten very close to our breastworks; where we was and below they hadn't gotten halfway yet. But they still came on.

I ran down along our line again, shouting, "Aim and shoot! Aim and shoot, fellows!"

The men at the breastworks at the clearing seemed to have settled into a regular pattern of shooting and then I realized we might need cartridges pretty quickly, so I had Sanford Van Dyke—who had been hit in the hand, but not so bad—see how much ammunition the men really had. If they ran out, there would be nothing left to do but retreat. At the clearing, the men were down to ten or fifteen rounds each, so we didn't have much time. I sent Develois Stevens scampering to find ammunition.

Next I went back to where my men was and checked to see how much ammunition they had. Forty to fifty rounds each, I discovered. I also found that the forward lines had begun to fall back and I assumed they was running short of ammunition. Just then I remembered something Sgt. Donoghue had told me at Gettysburg and I said to Asa Rich, "Go around to the dead and wounded and gather up their ammunition and give it out over at the clearing."

After this my recollection becomes somewhat of a swirl with a lot of blank spaces. I was told that Maj. Pettit was killed somewhere up the line, cut in half by a shell. His aides was barking out the orders in his place — but I was wondering when they would realize this spot was lost — because without a lot more ammunition and reserves it was most certainly lost — and hoping they wouldn't wait so long that we couldn't get out and back to the rest of the army — wherever it was. Of course, this was Maj. Pettit's group and they didn't like to leave a fight.

I also remember seeing the men in front still coming back to us. That's about when I noticed that one of the cannons on my line was shorthanded and I started toward it, thinking to help out — and then the earth around me opened up with a deafening roar. I felt myself lifted into the air and tumbling over and over and when I came down everything went black and quiet for me — tho I don't remember hitting the ground at all.

That is all I remember of the fight. I guess I was knocked out by the explosion or by landing on my head and it was a while — hours maybe — before I am sure I heard a noise behind me — the rumble of cavalry, most likely. Far off but clear enough to freeze my hand til the danger passed. Since I was ordered to keep a record of what happened — and since there is nothing else to do while I wait — I will continue my story where I stopped: After being tossed around by the explosion it was a good deal of time before I became aware of anything. First came the horrible, strangled braying of a wounded mule, calling and calling and calling—then I heard the moans of the wounded and the sounds of fighting—far, far away and nothing but a distant grumble. And barking. I heard barking and knew Spirit was near.

My face was mashed into the ground and when I blinked my eyes open I found myself staring at leaves and twigs and clots of dirt. It was dark by this time, but I could see enough to know that the fight was over here—the ground had that chewed-up look and there was some bodies near, just shapes so I didn't know who they was. Then came the voices—real ones—so I stayed still and listened.

Turned out to be a couple of Rebs searching the bodies for boots, food, and cartridges. They was whispering—which told me they was on the sneak and should be somewhere else, probably where the fight was. I played dead, as they went on whispering and shopping. Spirit barked and barked and then he set to growling. I wanted to look to see what was happening, but didn't. Next I heard a yelp and I supposed one of the Rebs kicked Spirit. When they had found all that they needed, they drifted off and the area around me was still except for the groans of the wounded and the cries of that mule.

That is when I moved my legs to see if they worked and got my left arm out from under my body, tho I moved slowly and quietly in case other Rebs was near. I could hear cavalry going up the path and some wagons and assumed they was Rebs—but it was dark enough and I was far enough away that if I was careful, I could slip away and avoid being taken prisoner.

I rolled onto my side next and pushed myself into a kneeling position. My head and arm and chest was on fire with pain but my legs seemed fine enough. I knew I could get clear as long as my legs held out. When I stood, I was so dizzy I swayed and had to lean against a tree for a while. This gave me a chance to glance all around.

I could just see the clearing thru the tree branches and bushes, not clearly. Just a lighter patch of gray. And the breastworks—solid and straight in places, ripped up in others. And some bodies and twisted up pieces of artillery. One soldier was on his back, his arm frozen as it was reaching up. For what? Help?

I didn't see any movement anywhere. The moans was away from me, in the clearing mostly. I thought about going around to see who was injured and who was killed—Lt. Toms wants a careful record of such. Then I thought better. The section was empty now, but it might take a while to find them, and the Rebs might be back any minute. And what could I do to help them? I didn't even have any water. I had to get away and do it while my legs had strength to carry me and my brain still worked. But which way?

The path was out of the question—too busy with enemy patrols. Our Army—if it still existed—was up toward Chancellorsville or thereabouts, but since the Rebs had broken thru the line, that way would be swarming with them. So I had to go in the safest direction—which was across where the Rebs had been when the fight started and deeper south into the woods.

Before setting off, I looked up and down my line as quickly as I could. I thought about Johnny then, so I went—hobbled, really—to where he had been. "Fort Henderson" was empty, and when I felt around I didn't find any signs of blood. Johnny might be a prisoner or he might have made it back to the main army, but at least he wasn't dead and that would please Sarah and her mother and sisters. That got me thinking about Sarah, wishing I had a picture of her—and it was then I noticed a strange shape down the line.

What I found was like a vicious punch to the stomach. Thinking about it even now makes me feel sick. Willie Dodd—who was the last holder of Lucky Minié—was sprawled on the ground, arms flung out, his right leg bent up at an awkward angle under his body. And on his chest was Spirit—dead, run thru with a bayonet by one of the Reb looters I'd heard prowling about earlier.

I wanted do so something for Willie and Spirit—take care of them somehow, maybe bury them proper or say some prayers. Maybe go look for those Rebs and—But I suddenly felt weak and light-headed, and my legs seemed as if they might buckle under me. Besides, a cavalry unit was thundering along the path in my direction.

I climbed over our breastworks and wandered toward the dark woods, past where A and C Companies had made their fight, past where the Rebs had had their advance pickets. There was dead soldiers to step over in these woods, some I could see was ours, some theirs.

I made a frightful amount of noise for someone trying to sneak away, but the cries of the wounded and that mule covered my clumsiness. I stopped to rest when the woods suddenly got thicker and turned to look back over the battlefield—and found it swallowed up by the black of night, still and sad. I couldn't see anything, not really, but it was all there in my head any-way. What was it Lt. Toms had said after Capt. Clapp had visited him that day last November—that this would be our deliverance?

My legs felt heavy and then I tripped and fell, and it took a time before I could push myself up. When I looked, I saw that I'd tripped over a severed leg.

And a voice started in—not Uncle's this time, but mine. It was another Bible line, one that I'd liked the sound of and wrote often, trying to picture the brave soldiers doing their noble work. I'm not sure how much I like those words now, but they seem to fit what happened. "Horsemen charging, flashing sword and glittering spear, hosts of slain, heaps of corpses, dead bodies without end—they stumble over the bodies!"

I was half a mile out and already feeling lost when I remembered seeing Spirit's body lying across Willie and I thought: They didn't have to kill that little dog. He didn't do anything to them but bark. He didn't have to die, and my eyes clouded up some as I left my friend and his dog and all the others behind and limped deeper into the Old Wilderness.

Later

I had just finished the last entry when a bunch of Rebs rode up and dismounted on the hill behind me. I thought they had sniffed me out, but then they commenced to jabbering away and laughing about how the Federals had run. Can't be talking about *our* Company—no one ran that I saw. Not even Theron Chrisler. They didn't seem to be nosing around for strays like me, so I relaxed some—til I smelled the coffee.

My stomach began growling then and reminding me it hadn't been fed in—who knows? Pulled leaves from the bush covering my little space and stuffed them in my mouth—bitter but got the juices going and the growling simmered down. Closed my eyes and chewed—thinking about poor Willie and Spirit, and Sgt. Donoghue, who must be dead, too, and Johnny and the others. I even thought about Shelp and hoped he'd gotten away.

I wanted to read Sarah's letters, but I didn't dare take them from my pocket because of the noise they would make. So instead I thought about Sarah and wondered if she was thinking about me.

That's what I did til the Rebs finished their coffee—probably got the coffee from us!—and packed up and rode away. Must leave. This section is as busy as the plank road.

Night

Dark. So dark can't see what I write, but am wide awake and will write any-way. Left last "home" when sun went down—moved deeper into Reb country. Clouds covered the moon and stars, so I walked where the walking seemed easiest. Went on—became confused—went on some more. Stepped into a stream—stopped to drink. Continued journey, slipping several times and getting caught in a sticker bush that scratched my hands, neck and face. Headache not as bad but it is still with me and wrist and leg are sore. Now at edge of field and will bed here—with biting bugs as company. Peaceful except for insect noise and some animal calls in the dark and my thoughts. Where is everyone I know? How are the Lt. and Caesar? Who else was hurt—or killed? How is William Kittler? I did not recall seeing him at all during the fight, but he must have been there. What is Sarah doing now? Sleeping peacefully most likely, with no idea at all of what has happened to us.

May 8 ?

Woke to sound of men working in the field. I counted four Negroes and thought to approach them—Caesar said they was all "kindly disposed to the Federal soldiers and would be truthful about roads and trails." But then I saw a white girl, riding toward them, cradling a musket, and I changed plans. They was far off, so I moved along the edge of the field unseen. But to where?

Tried to orient myself according to sun and thought about battle map and Caesar's finger moving across it. Head is still foggy and map remains unclear—but Caesar did say over here we would find "poor soil, poor farms, poor and mean white folk."

Stomach gave a shout about then, but all I could feed it was thoughts about my last real meal. A bit of hardtack would be a welcome feast just now, but gnawing on a stick is all I can do. Good thing there are so many streams in here or I would have no hope of escaping.

Can barely read last night's scribble. Wonder if the Lt. would change his mind about me keeping the journal if he ever saw that?

Later

Walked a little and find myself very nervous every time I come to a path or trail. Have heard patrols roaming the woods, thankfully far off. One time I came very close to two men arguing over who had eaten the most chicken and assumed they was a Reb patrol. No one else argues so loudly about food as soldiers do.

My head spins from hunger while my stomach agrees with growls. Kicked over a rotted log and saw it swarm with crawling creatures — a fine meal for some. Thought about it for myself, but then I gagged and so I guess I am not *that* hungry. Not yet any-way.

Skirted two fields after the first, both empty. Then I smelled food — close by and inviting — a stew with beef and potatoes my nose told me — and when my stomach learned this it set to churning and complaining! So I went toward the smell just to see.

What I found was a small cabin surrounded by a

neat little garden that was just beginning to turn green. Smoke from the cook fire was pouring from the stone chimney and bringing me that delicious smell. I was standing there breathing in "dinner" when the door opened and a white woman came out. I ducked when I saw her, not knowing what to expect, and she went right to her garden, where she cut some greens and then went back inside.

"There is food in there," I told myself, "and a bed." These thoughts made my legs tremble—I was only 200 feet away—so close I could imagine the food, feel the soft mattress. Surely she would not refuse me. Besides, there did not seem to be a man around—with so many gone to fight, this is a land without a lot of grown men—so I could always take what I wanted, even without a weapon.

Very tempting. But then a voice in my head—yes, *another* voice not my own—said, "Think it thru first." It might have been the Little Profeser who said this to me long ago—who can remember? Any-way, the voice added, "You don't want to act too quickly, especially when there are people around who want to do you harm." And she might be one—probably is one.

So I started wandering away—still taking in the smell—when there was a familiar loud report of a mus-ket behind me and a second later a ball sailed over my head and took a bite from the side of a tree. I didn't hesitate, but started to run—only my sleeve got snagged on a branch and I couldn't get it free at first. I tugged hard, snapped off the branch and tore my uniform, and started to run—tho I am not sure most folks would see it as running I was so clumsy and tired.

It was the white woman who shot at me and it was her who commenced shouting—cussing me to get off her land, calling me all kinds of terrible names and hollering that she'd seen a Yankee and so forth. But I didn't mind her yelling. As long as she was yelling, she wasn't reloading.

When I was out of her sight, I stopped to catch my breath, leaning heavily against a tree. Then I heard a second shot fired, followed a little time later by another—signal shots to alert her neighbors about trouble, I guessed. I pushed myself away from the tree and headed down a rocky hill. When I reached the bottom, I heard another alarm gun to my right answer the woman's, soon followed by another from over here, and then another from over there, and another and another. A number of dogs started in barking, too. All around me it seemed. I have heard musket fire many times since becoming a soldier, but I must say I have never felt as small and as helpless as I did just then. Hurried on, listening and looking and nervous every step.

It is now late in the day and I am near a small clearing with two log shacks in it—tobacca drying shacks, I think, because they are so tall, with some smoke seeping from the cracks near the roof of one. A while back, the door opened and an ancient Negro woman came out to gather up dead sticks. She's in there now, alone I think, and I am here writing this, waiting for darkness and asking myself silly questions—will she be "kindly disposed" toward me or will she turn me in? Will she have any food to spare? They are silly questions because I know I can't delay. I need food and I need rest and I need them now. I hope this will not be my last entry in this journal!

May 9

Yes, it is another day. Sunrise to be exact, and I have just opened my eyes from a sweet, long sleep. I intend to write a little and then be on my way. About last night—I put away the journal and began inching toward the shack, every step slow and deliberate, my heart thumping nervously.

At the edge of the clearing I paused to look and listen carefully. I'd made some sort of mistake with that white woman—a noise, a movement—and it nearly cost me my life. I didn't want to do the same here. The woods was empty and quiet and so was the clearing.

No one was moving around in the dark.

I found a small pebble and tossed it at the door. It struck with a soft crack. Since I had heard it, some-one inside should have, too, only there was no answer. I threw another pebble, this time a little harder.

The woman replied in a language I didn't under-stand—other than it was a question of some sort. Not angry, tho. More like a cautious, "Who's there?" "A friend," I answered in a whisper. "Come out, please."

The door creaked open a bit and the woman peered out. I had moved out of the woods and closer to the door so she could see me full. "I'll not harm you," I said, taking a step toward her. "I need help." The door opened more—enough that I could see her face—hard and questioning—and her eyes—dark and suspicious. I could also see a small knife clutched in her hand, ready to go to work on me if I turned out to be unfriendly.

"I am unarmed," I said, and raised my hands so there was no mistake about this and even turned around once. "Food. All I need is some food. A little. Any you can spare."

She looked me up and down several times and I guess I must have presented a pathetic sight when I think on it—blown up in a bloody battle, dirt and powder burns on my face and clothes, two days strolling thru the woods, hiding in dirty holes, no food and only a little restless sleep. She shook her head several times and said something to me, tho what it was I do not know. She spoke French with a heavy Southern accent and seasoned with only a bit of American. When I asked her to repeat what she said, she waved her hands toward the woods as if to tell me to go away. If I had any doubts about what she meant, she made herself clear when she closed the door firmly.

I should have left her alone—I had no right to put her in danger. But I had no choice either, so I said, "Food is all I need. I'll lick the pot if that is all you have." And I would have, happily, I was so hungry and desperate. When she did not reappear, I said a little more loudly, "Please, I won't stay long."

That door stayed shut, and I did consider leaving. But when I looked around, the woods was so dark and deep that I went straight to the door and knocked several times. "Please, open up. I have some coins—not much, but they are silver." I fished in my pockets for the coins, but couldn't find them. I was getting impatient and maybe a little louder than I should have been, considering. I know I wished Osgood Tracy was there to use some of that French he knows to get me in. "They are here . . . somewhere. If I can't find them, maybe buttons from my uniform—"

Suddenly the door opened again and the woman

stuck her head out, shushing me to be quiet and not looking happy at all. After glancing around, I think she said, "Step up, step up. Hurry!" But for some reason I hesitated, so she backed into the shack and waved with her hand that I should come in.

I went inside and was happy to see no one else in there. A tiny fire burning on the dirt floor in one corner gave off some welcome warmth and a layer of thin smoke—tho no worse than the smoke in one of our stockade tents. I hardly noticed the smoke smell to be honest. I was taking in another smell—food!

The woman rummaged thru a burlap sack and came out with a stump of a candle that she lit and stuck into a potato on a tiny table. She spoke to me—again, I had no idea what she was trying to say—but then she patted a little bed next to the table and gestured that I should sit. When I had settled onto the bed—and, oh, didn't it feel comfortable!—she handed me a ladle of water, which was room warm, but tasted fine. Then she deposited a small kettle on the table and handed me a wooden spoon.

I had no idea what was in that kettle—maybe hen or rabbit or even squirrel—and I didn't care. I ate it and made as much noise as any table of ten soldiers gobbling down a home-cooked meal.

The candle didn't throw much light, but enough

that I saw into every corner of the room and its contents, which was not much. This rickety bed I was on, the table and a wooden chair—which the woman was sitting in—plus a few small sacks and barrels scattered around the dirt floor. While I ate and studied the room, the woman talked on and on.

A little I figured out, most I did not, so I just nodded and smiled—that is, between bites of food. At one point I thought, what a crazy loon she is for talking away when she knows I don't understand her. Then I remembered the many voices I'd had in my head and decided that if she was crazy, then I certainly was, too, and probably more so.

I finished up what was in the kettle and then my manners began to return. "Thank you," I said. "That was good. Thank you." She had never taken her dark eyes off me while I was eating—and her eyes were curious and nervous mixed. I knew she was scared. Not of me, but of being found hiding and feeding me, the enemy.

I stood up, prepared to leave. "I have to go now," I said. I pointed to the door. "Go. I have to go to my people. Can you point me to the Rapidan—" and then I must have wobbled some because she came over and made me sit again and even indicated that I should lay down and sleep. It would be all-right.

I did not fight her. I could not. I lay back and put my

head on a thin pillow that smelled of body oil and wild herbs and leaves and felt as heavenly as any hotel pillow could. She sat down again and blew out the candle.

"My name is James," I said. "James Edmond Pease. Tomorrow I have to get back to my company." She said something but I had to ask her to repeat it. She said firmly, "Sally, boy. Coll me Sally."

"Good night, Sally," I said. She didn't answer. Instead, she leaned back in the chair, staring at the fire that was more glowing embers than flame now. She was deep in thought. A few minutes later a faint smile creased her lips and she nodded several times and mumbled. "Yes, yes, yes." At least I think she said that, tho why I don't know. Then she began singing very softly. The words was foreign to me — French, I guess — but they was soothing and gentle and made me feel safe. I wanted to

Tobacca shacks — Sally's is the one closest. No matter how much I tried, I could not make them look as worn out as they really are.

say something, ask her some questions—like, if she was a slave, why was it she lived out here by herself?—but I didn't. I didn't want to interrupt her. It was the first time I remember ever being sung to sleep.

Later

When I finished writing last time, I sat back—I was outside leaning against the shack. Just then, there was the rumble of horses moving fast and coming closer. A Reb patrol? I wondered. I stood up, not sure what to do. I could scamper into the woods, but how far could I hope to get?

It was Sally who grabbed me by the arm and pulled me back inside the shack, where she motioned that I should stay in the corner behind the door. She made it clear that I was to sit there and be quiet. Then she started fussing over the kettle of corn mush she had sitting in the fire.

I had no choice but to obey, so I sat with my knees drawn up and my arms wrapped around them, making myself as small as possible. When the horsemen rode up just a few seconds later, Sally went to the door to talk to them.

There was six or eight of them I guessed and they was so close to the door that they nearly blocked out the light. The one I took to be the group's leader said, "Benjamin, you check that other shack there for signs of the Yank while I talk to Sally here." "Yes, Grandpa," the one named Benjamin answered in a squeaky, little-boy voice. This was no Reb cavalry unit. The old man said good morning to Sally in French, his voice a little breathless, but pleasant enough other-wise.

He and Sally started chatting away, him asking her questions and her answering. I had some notion about what was being said because the man used the word "Yankee" several times. At one point the leader's horse poked its nose in the door and nudged Sally, and I tensed up, expecting the animal to betray me somehow. Sally just patted the animal casually and spoke to it in a friendly manner.

I could hear the other horses snorting and tapping restlessly at the ground with their hooves, hear the squeak of the saddles, hear the riders talking. Most of the voices sounded young, like schoolboys out play-ing. "Nothing there, Grandpa," Benjamin said at last. "What's she saying, Bill?" another one of the group—an adult this time—asked after a while, obviously impa-tient with the conversation. "She says she ain't seen the Yank or heard any strange noises." "Do you trust her?" the man asked. "As much as you can trust any of 'm," Grandpa replied, and the group of riders all laughed.

"Anything else? That was a lot of talking for so little information, Bill." "Well," Grandpa said, "she did wonder if we'd like to take breakfast with her. Corn mush." "Breakfast!" the man said with obvious disgust. "Let's get out of here. This place stinks God-awful." Stinks? I inhaled—quietly—but all I smelled was smoke and corn mush.

Sally and Grandpa talked some more briefly—all very pleasant and matter-of-fact—and then I heard the riders turn and hurry off. They had not even bothered to check inside her shack—maybe because the door was wide open and she had been so calm and casual. I let out a sigh, while Sally went back to the kettle of corn mush.

"Thank you. For what you told those men," I said, but Sally shook her head as if to say it was nothing unusual and handed me a bowl of mush and pan bread with honey. We did not talk much while we ate, but when I finished I said, "Well, I should go now." I tucked this journal inside my shirt. "Is there a safe place in the woods where I can wait for dark?"—and after listening and checking carefully, I went outside and reckoned which way was north by the position of the sun. "If I go that way, will I come to the Rapidan?"

Sally stared at me a second—she seemed almost frozen—so I thanked her again and took a step away from her shack. That set her moving, because she flew out of that shack and was on me in a second, talking fast and shaking her head no and holding tight to my arm. I shook her off—I had never been held by a Negro before and I think it scared me some—but she latched on again and seemed even more upset. And this time I didn't shake her off.

I tried to ask her a question or two—what was the matter? Why couldn't I go? "Is it that old man?" I asked. "Those fellows on the horses?" I pointed to the hoof marks in the dirt around us. That gave me a pause, remembering all of the alarm fire that trailed me from that woman's home. Sally shook her head no and started talking again, all the while gesturing with her hands.

Of course, I didn't understand her, which made her impatient, but that was okay because I was impatient, too. I tried to leave again, but Sally held tight. Then she stopped talking and I could see her puzzling out how to tell me what she wanted to say. I knew she'd hit on something when her face lit up with a smile and she went and broke off a small, dead branch from a nearby tree.

The next thing I knew, she was drawing a big rectangle in the dirt and filling it in with the stars and bars. It wasn't the prettiest drawing I ever saw, but I could tell it was the Reb flag. "Rebs? Reb soldiers? Is that what you mean? There are soldiers around. Where?" She waved her hand in a wide arc that said they was every-where and then drew a map of the area.

The Lt. was right. She knew the surrounding land pretty well and even put in the location of big and small farms and buildings. At first I thought she was going to show me a trail out of there, and I was excited at the notion of getting back to the boys. But then she pointed to the Reb flag and started making Xs in various places. One. Two. Three. Four, et cetera, et cetera.

If I felt the alarm shots had nearly surrounded me, those Xs told me something even worse. Except for a few isolated fields like this one, Rebs was camped all around us. And there would be patrols and messengers and such traveling all over the place, too. I'd been lucky yesterday — very lucky! — to stumble thru and find Sally's. I wasn't sure I had enough luck in me to slip back thru again, especially during the daylight.

Sally must have seen how upset I was, because she began talking in an animated way — something about night and someone called Davie. "Who is this Davie?" I asked. "Will you take me to him?" It took some time to make myself understood, and some more time for me to understand that no, I wasn't going to Davie, he was coming to me. And that was all Sally would say.

After we scuffed out the drawings of the map and flag — and I have to say I liked kicking at that flag — Sally led me deep into the woods and pointed to a spot that would be my "home" for the day. She had put together a little sack of food—cheese, a good hunk of pan bread, a small cask of water, several turnips, and her knife. Then she left to work on the farm of the people who owned her. She made me to understand this with another map and by making believe she was scrubbing down a floor.

With Sally gone and us not trying to "talk," it is suddenly very quiet and still. So here I am, back in the woods and alone. Waiting.

Later, around 12 noon

Dozed off several times today with all sorts of people and thoughts and worries swimming around in my head. Woke when horses came thundering by on what I guess is a nearby road. I made myself as small as possible, expecting those riders to come charging into the clearing again.

When I heard the distinct sound of shouted orders, I knew it was soldiers. My first thought was, If I don't run and make them angry, they won't shoot me outright. But when they came into the clearing and approached the tobacca shacks, my second thought was, Stay calm, Pease. They don't know you're here, so don't do anything foolish. I pressed myself as flat as I could to that damp ground.

Sally had chosen this spot well. She had planted me some 400 feet from the clearing, in a section filled with rocks, fallen, rotting trees, nasty sticker bushes, and underbrush, plus a healthy stand of young and old trees. And everything was leafing out. Unless someone stumbled over me, I might be taken for a rock if I just held still.

It didn't take long for the patrol to reach the shacks. They was far away and the leaves made seeing difficult, but that was fine with me. I did hear the officer in charge say "Search 'm," tho his voice was very faint and had no urgency to it. I decided then that I was being too curious, so I put my head down among the carpet of leaves, closed my eyes, and listened as each door was thrown open and the soldiers reported.

"Empty, sir," the first shouted, "a few barrels and such. Big hole in the roof, too." Another voice said, "Someone's livin' in here, Lt. A nigger by the looks of it. No sign of the Yank, tho."

Knowing that they was searching for me made the hairs on the back of my head tingle and I wanted very much to open my eyes just then—to see if they had any notion where I was. But I pressed my eyes closed even harder and told myself to lie as still as a stump. It was quiet again and I had the feeling that there was a lot of Reb eyes scanning the woods for me. Don't move,

I told myself. Don't even breathe hard. Then, after what seemed like a long time, I heard that Lt. say, "They said she was crazy scared. Bet she just saw one of the field hands wandering past and thought she'd seen the whole Federal Army."

The men all laughed at that and a little while later they withdrew and I opened my eyes. The last thing I heard one of them say was, "They oughta burn those shacks down."

Later

Dark clouds have moved in and the air feels heavy. Rain is on the way. At least my achy head and sore body think so. An hour or so ago a pair of riders entered the clearing and slowly rode up to the shacks. Both boys carrying very tall muskets. Was one of them Benjamin? I stayed low again, but watched as they circled the buildings, obviously looking for something. Me? At each door one dismounted and checked inside. Then they left.

Have eaten all of the food Sally provided. She has been as generous as she could be with the little she has, but my stomach still complains. Read my letters several times, listened to riders moving along the road and fretted. Set to dozing and had a remarkable dream. I pictured myself on leave going to visit Sarah and her family and heard myself asking her to marry me!!! That "little" idea startled me awake. I wondered what right had I to think Sarah would want to marry someone like me and, if she did, how I could provide for her and children. I wanted a number of children because being an only one can be a very lonesome thing. Suddenly I had a lot of mouths to feed and no land or skill to do it with—which was even more worrisome. Then I thought, Well, James, you have survived a number of fights and even been made a sgt. over others, so maybe you are ready to be wed. Many older men have done a lot less with their lives and it didn't stop them.

Still later

The sky is darkening and a cold mist is falling. Where is Sally? Will she be back soon with Davie? Will she be back at all? Should I think about striking out on my own? A wet night would be good cover for my journey, but it is bad for my spirits. Uncertainty, doubt, fear, hope, impatience, and misgivings are my companions now.

Night

Sally came home at last!—and with her she brought more rain. She did not come out to me right away, and

I did not approach the shack—even tho I was soaked thru and shivering. She left the door open, so I could see her light the fire and begin putting together a meal as if I did not even exist. I could not help but think about that last day at Uncle and Aunt's farm and feel very blue. Then I told myself what I already suspected—she is just waiting to see if anyone has followed her before bringing me in. Besides no one who sings you to sleep would just forget about you.

A few minutes later she came to the entrance and stood there, checking all around and listening. Then she looked right to where I was and waved that I should come in.

When I got there, a little stew was just beginning to bubble and the smell was wonderful—and my stomach said so!—but that was not what was on my mind just then. "Where is Davie?" I asked. "Will he be here soon? I have to leave, Sally. Tonight."

Sally put a potato she was peeling—the one that held the candle—into the kettle and said something to calm me down. But I just kept asking her about Davie and saying I had to leave and such til she said something sharp and pointed to the table. I may be the one wearing a sgt.'s chevrons, but Sally is the one with an officer's command!

So I sat down and waited while the stew cooked

up, and then we ate it and not many words was passed between us. I was beginning to think I would finish my stew and just leave, when Sally got up and began putting what little food she had in a sack. So I was leaving after all.

I decided to write in the journal til Davie appeared and I was at this work when — without sound or announcement — a man stepped into the shack — followed by four other people — a woman and three children!

The man and the woman glanced at me, then commenced talking with Sally — and I could not figure out any of it — and all the while the three children looked me up and down suspiciously. At one point the man — who I took to be Davie — began studying me especially hard. He is an impressive man — I guess he might be thirty or thirty-five years old and over six feet tall and very strong looking, even fierce. But it is his eyes that speak loudest — they are dark, almost black, intelligent, and move so quickly that I am sure there is nothing that escapes his attention.

The woman was younger than the man while the children looked to range in age from five or six all the way up to ten. Suddenly everyone fell silent. "Am I going with him now?" I asked Sally, pointing to the man and then to myself. I assumed no one spoke American because the man said something to Sally in French and she said something back. He then turned to me and announced, "I am Davie, Sally's nephew. This is my wife, Martha, and these are our children." He spoke American with a southern accent, with some French there, too, but not so thick as to make understanding hard. "Sally says we will all be leaving just as soon as she speaks with the children." "We *all* will be leaving?" I asked. "All of us," Davie said gravely, pointing to the children, his wife, Sally, and himself. "We are all that is left of our family. Now come here, please, young sir. We have to prepare for the journey."

May 10, near dawn

It is hard to tell about last night, so many things happened. While Sally talked with Martha and the children, Davie got me ready by mixing up a fine batch of mud right there in Sally's floor and rubbing it all over my face and hands and even the brass buttons of my uniform. "Won't it be hard to get thru with all of them?" I asked Davie at one point. "Sally is telling them now what they must do," he said. "They will listen to her. And the rain will help."

That was true, about the rain. It was a cold, steady shower now — the kind of weather that drives most soldiers to find shelter. Still, trying to slip seven people past the Rebs would be pretty hard to do. And then there was Sally. "Will Sally be okay?" I asked. "Will she be able to make the journey? Those woods are fierce and—" Davie waved the questions away. "If any of us make it out, it will be Sally. Don't you go worrying about her, Sgt. Worry about yourself."

Sally finished talking with Martha and the children, then she turned to us and let out a soft laugh when she saw me. She said something to Davie, who also laughed. "She says the mud makes you look like her husband, who is gone ten years now. But she thinks you might be even scrawnier."

We left right after this, with Davie leading. The oldest child—who was a girl—was right behind her father. Behind the girl came Martha, who was holding the hand of a boy, while Sally followed them with the other child—a girl—in tow. I came last in our little parade.

"Come along," Davie said as he entered the woods by way of a tiny trail. I thought we would be in for a bad trip when the little girl became afraid and started whining and struggling to avoid entering the dark woods. That kind of action was okay here near the empty clearing, but if we was close to Reb soldiers, it could cost us dearly. Fortunately Sally gave the little girl's arm a hard tug and said something in her ear, and then we went on without a peep from either child.

Davie had moved ahead of us—about thirty or forty feet—so we could barely see him. He told us before leaving that we was to watch him carefully and to move when he moved, stop when he stopped.

He seemed to have a purpose for every step he took—at least I hoped so. The woods all looked the same to me, and without a moon or stars I had no idea what direction we was headed. Sally was right to make me wait—without a guide I would have been lost in no time or been scooped up by the Rebs.

If I had any doubts about this, they disappeared when we was about a half mile from the clearing. Davie suddenly stopped and did not move for a very long time. I could see him leaning forward, listening, and searching the woods. He heard or saw something, I was sure. But what?

Time dragged along while we waited, and the two littlest began pulling this way and that. Both Sally and Martha knelt beside the children, holding them tight and whispering to them.

At last Davie came back to us and whispered first to Sally and then to me that there was a small fire in the woods off to the right about 200 feet. Guards for the pasture where a sizable number of Rebs was camped, Davie guessed. If that was true, I told Davie, it meant that there was other guards positioned all around the field at regular intervals. "Is there another way?" I asked. Davie shook his head no and said this was the best route—there was another Reb camp to the left and the land to the right was too rough. We needed to get beyond the pasture ahead but he did not seem to know what to do next and commenced whispering with Sally and his wife.

"They will likely have little fires," I said, interrupting their talk. "On a rainy night, the officers will let them have fires to drive off the cold. And they will give a signal to say everything is O.K. Probably every fifteen minutes. That is how our guards work, any-way."

Davie told this to the others, then said we would wait for the next signal and if he felt it safe we would move ahead. Otherwise, we would have to go back and try another night. I was to carry the little girl, while he would carry the small boy—that way, there would be fewer feet to cause noise. I also told Davie that once we was past the ring of guards, we should angle to the left and then stop to listen again. There might be a second line of guards posted and they would signal at a different time than the first. "Sally was right," Davie whispered as he shouldered one of his children. "She said a sgt. in the army would know things that would help us. Even so young a sgt. She knew that the moment she saw you."

I must have looked startled by his words—I mean I don't believe I present a very military appearance just now—but Davie added, "It was in your eyes, Sgt. Sally can tell a lot by the eyes."

I picked up the girl and she immediately began reaching toward Sally, whimpering to be in her arms. My shoulder and arm hurt some where I'd landed on them, but that wasn't what bothered me most. I was thinking: This could be very bad for us, especially if the girl got loud. Fortunately Sally was right there, soothing and hushing her gently, so the girl did not struggle hard to get free of my arms.

What Sally said, I do not know. But I did hear the name Harriet several times, so I commenced whispering in Harriet's other ear and saying her name often, til she turned her big eyes on me and even reached out to touch my face and whisper something back to me. It was while we was whispering back and forth that I realized how light she was—a good gust could have sent her sailing like a leaf—and how thin her arms and legs really was.

Pretty soon, Harriet grabbed hold of my uniform and held tight. Around then, I heard a distant shout, and immediately it was repeated and repeated and repeated down the line of guards. The voices got louder and clearer as they approached, til we could hear the guards singing out, "All is quiet!" one after another.

The call was sounded just to our right, where Davie had seen the fire, and then—not more than 100 feet away!—it came again on our left. Then the call continued its journey, fading away to nothing as it went around the rest of the pasture.

Davie did not hesitate, but moved forward very slowly. Now was a time to be thankful for a rainy, moonless night, as we was as silent and as invisible as tiny night creatures trying to avoid the eyes of the owl. After we passed the first line of guards and went to the left, we halted again to listen. Not long after this, the same shouted signal could be heard sweeping around the pasture. Fortunately, the inside line was not spaced so tightly together, so it was easy to slip between the nearest guards.

We was now between the guards and the main camp, circling around the pasture in a bit of woods I would guess was 300 feet from the camp—enough that I could see where the woods gave way to open pasture, but could not see any tents or other army equipment. During all of the waiting Harriet fell fast asleep on my shoulder, her breath coming regular and warm, as if nothing in the world was wrong—and I was happy to have it so.

We traveled like this all the way around the pasture— a half a mile at least—and eventually we came to the spot where Davie wanted to cut off into the woods again. Which meant we had to go back thru the lines of guards once more.

This time we was aided not only by the regular call, but by the fact that a guard change took place just then. There was all sorts of commands being issued, men talking—mostly complaining that the change of guards was late, as usual!—and a general stomping and crashing thru the underbrush with some cussing. So we hunched down low and was past all of them in just a few minutes.

Davie picked up the pace a mite then and I assumed that meant there was no Rebs camped over here. So on we went—over fallen-down trees, around rocks, across little streams. In some sections the walking was easy, but just when I relaxed a little, some sticker bush would jab at me to remind me I wasn't safe yet. The sleeping Harriet had pulled her legs up and made her body into a ball, so carrying her even in the rough terrain was easy.

The land was thickly wooded and generally flat for nearly an hour, but then we came on a series of steep hills with lots of slippery rocks to climb. At one point Davie decided to walk up the middle of a cold, fast-moving stream, and we followed.

All of this was beginning to wear me down, my leg and arm being banged up as they was, and Harriet suddenly seeming to grow heavier. I started to breathe hard. How was Sally holding up? I wondered. How was

Martha and the oldest girl doing? But they all seemed fine. Fortunately for me, Davie stopped often to listen and to peer ahead into the darkness, which gave me time to rest. He seemed to be choosing particularly rough terrain for our travel, to avoid Reb patrols, I guessed. There was hardly any other life in here, for that matter. Even the animals stayed clear of these places.

We came to a narrow road and stopped to rest and taste some of Sally's food. Harriet and her brother slept on, while Sally, Martha, and the older girl looked as exhausted as I felt. "Are we far?" I asked. I did not want to walk another step if I did not have to, and besides, we had used up just about all of the night already.

Davie was working on some corn bread and looking up the road. "Far?" he said. "Not very far, I think." But he did not seem very sure of this. "Do you know where this road leads?" I asked. "North," Davie said, "I think it leads North." "You think?" I asked, and I am certain my voice sounded alarmed. "You mean you're not sure if this road goes North?"

Sally must have heard my upset because she and Davie and Martha began talking back and forth among themselves, pointing this way and that, sometimes up the road, sometimes into the woods behind us. Then Davie said, "Sally says the road goes North to a bigger road. She says if we follow the big road a few miles it will take us to a place where we can cross the river."

I thought about this a moment. The road was temptingly flat and I know my feet would welcome a few miles that did not include tree roots, large rocks, and streams. Then I thought better. "If the Rebs control the land above here," I said, "they will have guards posted in places. We should stick to the woods."

A heartbeat later—as if to prove me correct—we heard a rumbling that was already mighty close on us. I rolled over and partly covered the sleeping children. "Get down and stay still," I hissed, and soon we was all no more than lumps on the ground. And good thing, too. The rumbling—the sound of hooves, I now realized— was accompanied by the clink of metal on metal. Then the cavalry—Reb, I could just see—began going past our position, one after another after another, on and on, without end. 100. Maybe 200. Maybe more. After a while, I gave up looking at them and closed my eyes.

We was not more than fifteen feet from them, but Davie had selected a spot deep in shadow and the riders swept past us. If any glanced our way, they probably thought we was rocks or logs. Even after the line of horses ended and everything grew quiet again, we stayed on the ground without moving.

"That was close," I said when I finally got up and had

Harriet in my arms again. "Come along," was all Davie said. "No time to waste."

We was across the road—and we ran very quickly to the cover of the other side—and plunged into the woods. A little beyond the road we came to an empty field. "I think this is good," I said. I was remembering Caesar's finger moving over the map in Lt. Toms's tent and how he said there was more farmland along the Rapidan. We skirted this field and soon came to another and another. Then there was another section of woods and not long after this we came to a wide body of water—the Rapidan.

Davie took us up along the river several miles to where the ford was. Which army controls this area? I wondered. Fortunately, I heard a series of orders issued—all in a very comforting Northern accent.

At the ford, the guard challenged me just as soon as he heard us, telling me to halt and say the password. I answered by telling him who I was and what company I was a part of. "I have been lost in the woods since the 6th," I told him. "Come forward slowly with your hands raised," he ordered, and I did as ordered. "I would raise my hands," I said as I stepped from the woods, "but I have a child in my arms. And there are more with me. Five more."

He had his musket pointed at me as we approached,

and his eyes opened wide when he took in my appearance and then saw Sally and the others. "Damn if you don't look just like one of these niggers here," the guard said. I moved a few steps closer and turned to the side so he could see my sgt.'s chevrons. "These are my friends, Pte., and they saved my life. You will treat them with respect, do you hear?" "I didn't mean nothin' by it, Sgt.," he sputtered. "It's just that you look . . . well, you look—" "Never mind how I look, Pte. Take me to the officer in charge and be quick about it."

We was brought into camp then and left at the guard's tent with warm blankets to wrap ourselves in. I handed Harriet over to Sally—tho Harriet actually clung to me so it took some doing to pry her fingers loose. Next some tins of Army coffee appeared. Just as thick and old as any I have ever had—and just as delicious!

A bucket of water was produced and I washed as much of the mud from my face and hands as I could. The others was now huddled on a cot, wrapped tight in their blankets and sinking fast into needed sleep. Except Sally, that is. Harriet had gotten fretful, and Sally had her on her lap and was stroking her hair and humming.

After this an officer came to question me and I was happy to tell him about the Reb troops I'd seen near Sally's and the cavalry headed along the road. I tried to find out about the 122nd and my Company, but this officer was sour at being called out so late, and any-way he did not have much information about them. He did say that the fight in the woods had gone back and forth—first they looked to take the day and then us. He couldn't have meant where we was, since it was clear they had beat us badly there! The fighting swung to our favor after their Gen. Longstreet was wounded and had to leave the battle, but then Gen. Lee managed to get his army over to Spotsylvania before we did and was still there and still fighting. He didn't know exactly where our regiment was. They could be any-where between the Old Wilderness and Spotsylvania, or they could have even been pulled from the fight and put in reserve.

"You should get some rest, Sgt. And report to the adjutant's tent for duty in the afternoon." Report for what? I wondered. But that wasn't the most important thing on my mind just then. "What about these people, sir?" I asked. "They helped me escape." "We'll see about them tomorrow, Sgt. There are some empty tents over by the sutler's shanty you can use. The sgt. of the guard will show you where they are."

I thanked him, and then the sgt. came in and took us to our tents for the night. I was so tired, I do not even remember saying good night or thank you to Davie or Sally or any of her family. But there will be tomor-row for that. Tonight I am to sleep on a soft cot under a warm blanket—but first I will reread Sarah's letters one more time and pray for peaceful dreams.

May 11

Spoke with a Capt. Riskind around noon. He told me there was no way to know where G Company was at present and that til this was known I would be assigned to help unload ambulances. In the past this would have been just fine with me, being a safe occupation, but I protested this time—only the Capt. did not want to hear any of it.

I also told the Capt. about what Sally and Davie had done for me, and asked if they could get help from anyone. "There is a new group running around camp these days—the Union Commission, from up in St. Louis or there-abouts. I'll ask them what can be done." I thanked him and then took lunch—a mighty heap of it—and wrote Sarah a brief letter to tell her I am very much alive, and that I was sure Johnny was, too. After, I went to the field hospital to help with arriving ambulances.

The ambulances stream into camp day and night fully loaded. Most of the wounded are being transferred from regimental hospitals close to the fighting and have already been treated. Many others have been wandering about for days and have only now found their way to the surgeons. The surgeons here are very busy—prying pieces of metal from torn-up flesh and sawing off mangled bone.

I ask about the 122nd and G Company whenever I can, but no one—not the ambulance drivers, surgeons, nurses, litter carriers, or wounded—has any news of them. When he heard me asking these things, one of the other litter carriers said, "If you ask too often, you'll find them for sure, and then you will be back in it. I have been here four weeks and expect that I can stay, as long as I don't make too much noise."

I thought about what this soldier said all day. They certainly need help here, as the ambulances keep arriving. But the number of wounded tells me that they need help out there, too, and maybe more so.

Ambulance arriving with wounded.

7 o'clock

When my day was over, I went hunting for Sally and Davie and their family. It took a while, but I found them with some officers, all of them working at cleaning clothes and cooking and such. I arrived just as Sally was lecturing a capt. about leaving his clothes all about his tent, and the capt., who did not understand a word she was saying, just stood there nodding his head while his friends laughed at the scene. Davie said they had traded one dirty house for another, but at least here they can leave when they want. And it seems they will be doing just that in two or three weeks, according to Davie. A representative from the Union Commission said a train would take them to St. Louis, where the group has its head-quarters and is helping the refugees from the South.

Sally brought us bowls of potatoes, carrots, and beef—much different food from what we had just a day ago! While we ate, I asked Davie and Sally some of the questions that had come into my head—like where Sally had come from that she speaks French and not American? Davie told me, "Sally is from an island off the coast of South America. She and her sister was taken and sold to people living outside of New Orleans when Sally was seven. It was a big place and the white folk was decent enough, but then Yellow Jack fever came and lots of people died. My mother and father and brother's family. Sally's husband, too. Even our master's wife — that was when he decided to leave, so his two children would be safe from Yellow Jack — and Sally raised such a fuss til he brought us all to Virginia. We was in Virginia ten years when you come along." I asked if they had ever considered running North before now, and Davie said, "We considered it every day — even before the war — but Sally said no, we had to wait for the right time. Sally said you wanted to get back to your soldier friends something bad and knew you would, too. And so would we if we went along. She could tell you did not give up easy."

We talked more, mostly about what they did — which sounded a lot like what I did on Uncle and Aunt's farm! Except that I was never beat, no matter how bad things got, and I could leave and not worry that any-one would hunt me down.

Seems that Sally was such a talker and so stubborn that her owner thought the house might be quieter — and the other Negroes less "agitated" — if she wasn't around all the time — which is why he let her live apart in the abandoned tobacca shack. I told them that I had included them in my journal and I took it out to show them. Sally spotted the minié-ball hole and touched it, looking from it to me. Then her face brightened and she spoke to Davie. "Sally says she is proud to be in your

156

book. She said your words must be very strong to stop a musket ball like that."

May 12

I think some would call it a miracle. Today I was helping with the wounded when I heard a voice say, "Sgt. Pease, we all thought you dead and gone!" It was Pete McQuade, who had bandages on both his hands, his right leg, and parts of his face, and he looked to be thinner besides.

He told me that after I was "killed"—because that is what everyone thought—wave after wave of Rebs came over and Maj. Pettit's men finally called retreat. Most of those who could move themselves made it back to the main road, where the officers rallied them. They went up the road and joined the fight again, but then the woods caught fire and forced them to retire a second time. That is where Pete got shot in the leg and then the fire burned him as he was crawling off. "The Company's been shot up bad, Sgt.," he added, tho he didn't remember exactly who had been killed or wounded. I asked about Johnny, and Pete thought him fine the last he remembered seeing him. "But the fighting has moved over near Spotsylvania and is very hot, I heard. They was headed for the Ny River, last I saw them."

I told Pete I would be going over there myself just

as soon as I could break free from my duties here. Pete said he thought they could use my help, and then he told me to fetch something from his vest pocket that I should keep. It was a coin—the silver coin Sarah had sent me for good luck and which I gave to Pete a while back. "This didn't do you much good, Pete," I said. "Oh, but it did," Pete replied. "I count myself lucky to have gotten out at all. A lot didn't."

I tucked the coin into the pocket with Sarah's letters, thanked Pete, and went back to my work. Later I found the officer in charge and told him I knew where my Company was and wanted to go back to them, but he said I would have to wait til orders was issued officially. I said it was important that I get back to them, but he said it was important to wait for the signed papers to come thru. "Otherwise we will both be in trouble, Sgt.," he explained. "Gen. Grant is cracking down on stragglers and such, and he is a man who means business."

I thought about what this officer said while I helped move the wounded from the ambulances to the surgeon's tent. Sgt. Donoghue always said, "An order is an order, and it isn't our job to go question them either." That is true, I believe, but I do not recall the officer "ordering" me to stay in camp, and I have certainly not heard from Gen. Grant directly. So I have decided to leave—before anyone gets around to ordering me not to!

May 13

Said a tearful good-bye to Sally and Davie and the others, and thanked them over and over for helping me and wished them well in St. Louis. Next I found Pete McQuade and told him what I was doing. Then I hitched a ride out of camp on an ambulance, which took me up the road several miles. Have walked ever since — the roads being less congested at night, tho still busy with supply wagons going and coming, cattle being taken to the army for food, and ambulances, of course. The ambulances never seem to rest.

Came upon some soldiers having breakfast at sunrise and was invited to join them — for $1! These fellows had been near the center of the line of battle on the morning of May 6 and had been pretty well licked by the Rebs, too. When I asked one of them which was the fastest way to Spotsylvania Court House, he just shook his head and said, "Take my word for it, Sgt. You don't want to go over there. It is a living Hell." When I said I did, he handed me his musket and cartridge box and said, "You will need these more than me then. I am going home!"

His rifle felt heavy to me, not having held one in many days — heavier than I remember and much heavier than little Harriet. I had to smile when he wished me "good shooting."

Later

I am down to the last pages of this journal—who would have believed I would be alive to say that—and so I must choose my words carefully. The road has been very busy as I get closer and closer to the fighting. Early in the afternoon I heard the rumble of the big siege guns in the distance. The sound of artillery grew louder and stronger, booming and booming away, and when I pictured them—and what they could accomplish!— my legs wobbled some.

Came to several cutoffs in the road, with streams of men and wagons heading up them and away from the fighting. The crackle of musket fire could be heard now, too, mingling with the rumbling thunder of the cannons. I have to admit that I thought a second or two about turning up one of those roads and disappearing into the crowd. Most everyone thinks me dead, so I probably wouldn't be missed.

But then I thought about Sally—who helped me when she really did not have to and put herself at risk. And Harriet. How many other Harriets are there waiting still for our help? And I thought about Johnny—who is like a brother to me—and Lt. Toms and the rest of the boys. I even thought about Charlie Shelp, who is as cussed as they come and no friend of mine, but I think I can handle him just as I can handle Reb sharpshooters, my

160

curse, and Army coffee. And there is Sarah, too—who I never want to disappoint. Ever.

Which got me to thinking. When I left Uncle and Aunt, I left nothing and headed toward nothing. Now I am heading toward people who count on me and need me, even if just a little. I will probably never be a very brave soldier, but I think I can do my job and do it in an honorable way. And after this war is over? Who knows?

I looked up just then, and there, not many feet in front of me, was a capt. on horseback staring right at me. He had a crisp uniform, a perfectly clipped mustache, sat very straight on his horse—and seemed to be the sort who did not take much none-sense. When I was closer, he called out to me in a sharp voice, "Where are you going, Sgt.?"

I will tell you that my heart jumped a beat and my blood ran cold, thinking I had been caught absent without permission and would have to pay the price. But then I gave the Capt. a sharp salute like those the Lt. gave to the Capt. delivering our orders each morning. "I have deserted my post at the field hospital, sir," I said, "and I'm heading to Spotsylvania and the fighting." The Capt. looked at me a moment, trying to figure out if I was lying or just crazy. "What is your name, Sgt.?" he asked. "I am Sgt. James Edmond Pease, G Company, the 122nd Regiment, New York Volunteers, from Onondaga

County, sir. But I did not volunteer to carry stretchers."

The good Capt. looked at me closely, and I am certain he decided then I was indeed crazy. But he just smiled at me and said, "Then you had better hurry along, Sgt. They will be needing you about now." "Yes, sir," I said. I then turned to go on my way when the Capt. called out, "Oh, and Sgt., good luck to you." "Thank you, sir," I replied, "But I believe I have all the luck I will need."

Epilogue

James located what remained of G Company near Spotsylvania Court House late in the day of May 13. He was warmly greeted and happy to be among familiar faces, but sad to see so many fewer of them. He learned then that the recent fighting had taken the lives of four of his comrades besides Willie Dodd and Spirit: Sgt. Donoghue, Niles Rogers, Lyman Swim, and Cornelius Mahar. Another twelve had been wounded, though only six had serious injuries: Lieutenant Toms, Otto Parrisen, Hudson Marsh, Benjamin Breed, Pete McQuade, and James Wyatt.

James had little time to mourn the loss of his friends. Confederate General Robert E. Lee had control of the land around Spotsylvania, and Union General Ulysses S. Grant was determined to have it — at any cost. By the time James arrived, Union forces had already spent several brutal days attacking strong Rebel defensive positions, but had failed to break through Lee's lines. James and G Company were in the thick of it every day until May 23 — with James recording what happened in a brand new journal — when they were finally given two weeks' furlough.

Free to do what he wanted, James accompanied Johnny to the Henderson farm in New York State. "We had a needed rest," James wrote, "and I was able to meet many of Johnny's friends and relatives, as well as Sarah." The young couple's meeting went extremely well for both of them, and on June 4, James and Sarah were wed in the local Episcopal church.

The celebration had barely ended when James and Johnny found themselves back in Virginia and in the middle of the fighting once again. G Company would take part in several major battles before the end of the war, including action at Cold Harbor, Petersburg, Cedar Creek, and Appomattox Courthouse. When Robert E. Lee finally surrendered his army, on April 9, 1865, James's Company had been reduced to just twenty men, the rest either dead, wounded, or taken prisoner. At the time he left the Army, James was seventeen years old and had risen in rank to second Lieutenant.

It was during these final months of fighting that a sketch artist from *Frank Leslie's Illustrated Newspaper*, Francis Schell, spotted James drawing in his journal. Schell thought James's work showed great promise and suggested he send samples to his boss. Soon James began submitting sketches of soldiers in camp, on the march and in battle, several of which were reproduced in *Leslie's*. He became a staff artist for *Leslie's* at the close of the war and covered such important stories as the building of the transcontinental railroad, the exploration and settlement of the West, and the Indian Wars. Sarah accompanied James on these assignments and eventually wrote articles of her own. Sarah and James had one child, Kate.

As for the veterans of G Company, they met every year at the reunion of the 122nd New York Volunteers, where they exchanged recollections of the war and brought each other up-to-date on their lives. Johnny Henderson did indeed marry the girl from the neighboring town and became a successful farmer, but he was best remembered for spinning tall tales about the Civil War. His favorite was about the time James charged ahead of everyone else and drove off several hundred Confederate soldiers single-handedly.

Osgood "Little Profeser" Tracy went back to medical school and became a doctor with a successful practice in Albany, New York, while Washington Evans became a skilled carpenter and helped to construct some of the most beautiful mansions in Syracuse. Charlie Shelp took his fiery, no-nonsense personality west, first as a foreman on Union Pacific Railroad work gangs and later as manager of a fur-importing company in San Francisco.

But of all the personal stories, the most intriguing was that of the notoriously shy William Kittler. William was wounded in the leg by an exploding shell at Cold Harbor, but he refused medical treatment for several days despite the obvious pain. Infection set in, followed by a high fever, during which William became unconscious and was finally rushed to the surgeons. It was there, while having his uniform cut from his body, that William's secret was revealed—William Kittler was in fact a woman! Her real name was Gabrina Sales, and she had cut her hair short and joined the army in the same patriotic fervor that had gripped most of the men and boys. She was discharged from the Army and shipped North to recover and no one from G Company ever heard from her again. Rumor had it, however, that a soldier looking remarkably like William Kittler—and limping noticeably—had been spotted during the fighting at Appomattox.

As for Lt. Toms, he recovered from his wounds and returned to lead G Company in January 1865, when the Army laid seige to Petersburg, Virginia. He was repeatedly passed over for promotion during the rest of the war, despite a clean record and many heroic acts. After being severely wounded at Fisher's Hill, Virginia, he was discharged from the Army still with the rank of lieutenant. He returned to his hometown and family, where he took up his old position as schoolteacher.

James made several attempts to find out what had

happened to Sally and her family, but was never successful. He did, however, receive a letter from a former volunteer for the Union Commission, the civilian organization in St. Louis that helped relocate many refugees from the war. While there were no records of where individuals had been sent, the volunteer recalled that a number of former slaves had been given farmland in the Dakota Territory near the Canadian border. Letters to the area received no reply.

James returned to the United States briefly in 1910 to attend the forty-fifth anniversary celebration of the end of the Civil War. Many of his comrades from G Company had passed on by then, leaving just a handful to remember the men and boys who had fought to preserve the Union. James died of a heart attack four years later while staying on Palawan Island in the Philippines; Sarah died ten years after James while on assignment for *National Geographic* in New Zealand.

Almost a year after the death of her mother, a steamer trunk was delivered to Kate Pease's home in Montana. Inside were the personal effects of her parents. At the bottom, carefully wrapped in a hotel towel were her father's Civil War journals. The final entry in the second journal reads:

"June 5, 1865: Well, the war is over and we have made it thru alive! Johnny and I will walk home tomorrow, but today will be spent in saying good-bye to friends and having our last—I hope!—Army supper. Because Lt. Toms is at home recovering, I will take these journals with me and hold them til he decides to write his history of G Company. I only hope that something I say here will be of use to him, tho I don't see how the words of a scared boy could interest him—or anyone else—very much. As I end this entry I believe I can truly say that *now you have read it all.*"

Stuck in the back of the journal was a small, yellowing envelope with a tarnished silver coin inside. On the envelope was written: "Luck is measured by the friends you make and the people you love."

Life in America
in 1863

Historical Note

On April 12, 1861, Confederate cannons under the command of General Pierre G.T. Beauregard opened fire on Federal forces at Fort Sumter. With this act, the Confederate States of America — which would number eleven states from the South after the fall of Fort Sumter — declared war on its Northern counterpart. The war (referred to as a revolution in the South and a rebellion in the North) would last four bloody years and cost the lives of an estimated 600,000 soldiers.

At the heart of the Civil War was the issue of slavery and whether each state had the right to decide for itself if slavery would be permitted within its borders. To white Southerners, slavery — and control of its 3,860,000 black slaves — was crucial both economically and culturally. They insisted that their farming economy could not survive and prosper without the cheap labor provided by slaves. Besides, they claimed, blacks were inferior and needed to be watched over and cared for by their white masters.

Most Northern states had already banished slavery and were pressing for its abolition in the rest of the United States and in the two million square miles of land west of the Mississippi. White Southerners viewed abolition as arrogant and a direct threat to their traditions and way of life. After decades of political wrangling, court cases, and compromises, the issue came to a head with the election of Abraham Lincoln as President in 1860.

Lincoln had declared himself firmly opposed to slavery and its introduction in the western territories, but he was willing to let it exist and die a natural death in states that already sanctioned it. His position did not appease Southerners, especially since a majority of the newly elected Congress was firmly antislavery. It would not be long, proslavery advocates warned, before the new President and his Congress flexed their political muscles and placed more and more restrictions on slavery. They had to act quickly before it was too late. And so, on December 20, 1860, South Carolina passed an ordinance of secession, proclaiming that the union previously existing between it and the other states was dissolved. Within weeks, six other Southern states adopted their own ordinances of secession.

This move took Lincoln and most Northerners by complete surprise; the bombardment of Fort Sumter three and a half months later sent them into action. Lincoln put out an urgent call for 75,000 volunteers—the first of many such calls—to defend and maintain the Union.

Meanwhile, a second wave of secession strengthened the Confederacy, and broadsides and newspaper ads proclaimed the need for able-bodied soldiers.

Men on both sides rushed to sign up. Would-be soldiers crowded the recruitment centers in large cities or signed on with locally organized units. Emotions ran so high that enlistment quotas were surpassed everywhere. Caught up in the fervor of the moment were boys from both the North and the South.

No one actually knows how many boys were able to join their side's army. Record keeping (when it existed at all) was extremely sloppy at the time, and enlistment procedures were so lax that most boys who claimed to be eighteen — which was the legal age of enlistment at the opening of the war — were allowed to sign up unchallenged. One study made by the U.S. War Department at the close of the nineteenth century estimated that of the 2,100,000 who served in the Union Army, over 800,000 were seventeen years old or younger. Of the 850,000 soldiers the Confederacy sent into battle, between twenty and thirty percent were underage.

Why these boys were so eager to join varied a great deal. Of course, many boys knew what the issues were and willingly put their lives at risk for their beliefs. But a surprising number had little notion or understanding of the political and social implications of the war. They had simply been caught up in the "war fever" that swept the country and wanted to be a part of what they thought would be a brief but glorious adventure. Others enlisted hoping army life would be an exciting alternative to the routine of endless farm chores back home. Still others signed on for no better reason than because their friends had, or because they didn't want to appear cowardly or sympathetic to the enemy.

While their motives for enlisting differed, these boys did have one thing in common: They loved to write. Almost every soldier sent letters home, and a surprising number kept detailed journals of their experiences. Usually, their writing styles were direct and simple, and their spelling was often highly creative. What is more, they tended to focus on the everyday events of army life — the bad coffee and lack of food, the tedious daily routine, the hours of marching, and their actions in battle. Yet it is through this intense focus on details that they are able to bring this war so fully alive for us today.

After four years of civil war, after the loss of hundreds of thousands of lives and a massive destruction of property, the Union was indeed restored and the slaves were freed from their bondage. Gone, too, was the idea that any state or collection of states could decide to break free of the others or that the federal government was subservient to the states. In its place emerged a stronger central government, one that would orchestrate the taming and settling of the vast West, become a majority world power, and play a larger and larger role in the lives of its citizens.

The Civil War also changed the boys who fought in it. It robbed them of their childhoods, forcing them to confront a hateful and violent adult world. But like the Union they fought for, those who survived came out stronger for their scars and wiser for their experiences.

The Civil War began on April 12, 1861, when the Confederate army opened fire on Union forces at Fort Sumter in South Carolina. Early in the war, volunteers on both sides rushed to join up, for reasons ranging from the defense of their homelands to the assurance of a pair of boots and dinner. The Union soldiers often wore kepi hats, with flat, round tops and stiff visors, like the ones worn by French soldiers.

TO ARMS!
RALLY FOR THE RIGHT!
Recruits Wanted
For THREE MONTHS SERVICE, IN

COMPANY A
GRAY RESERVES
CAPT. CHARLES S. SMITH.

ARMORY,
810 MARKET STREET,
UP STAIRS.

To reinforce the regular army, President Lincoln asked for 75,000 volunteers to enlist for three months' service, as advertised in this recruiting poster. Few were prepared for the ensuing four-year conflict.

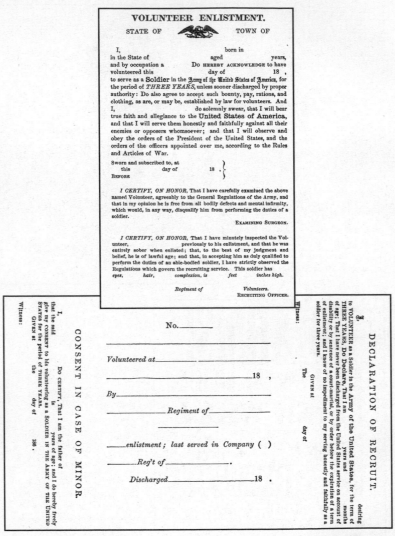

Each volunteer for the Union army completed an enlistment form (top), and a Declaration of Recruit form (bottom). The legal age for soldiers was eighteen, but some as young as ten years old lied about their ages in order to be allowed to fight.

After individual companies learned drills, commanders held mass drills to teach maneuvers within larger units of regiments and brigades.

In its exposed position, the Gettysburg headquarters of Major General George Meade became the center of a terrible artillery fire on July 2, 1863. Several soldiers were killed, forcing Meade, the Commander of the Army of the Potomac, to abandon the building.

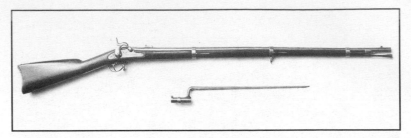

The Springfield musket was the preferred weapon of most soldiers, but it was long (58 inches), heavy (almost 10 pounds), and difficult to use. Even the best soldiers could not load and fire more than three shots per minute. The development of the M1861 Rifle Musket, pictured here, allowed for more shots and a farther range, which forced the offense to a longer charge subject to heavier fire and, therefore, greater losses.

The battles of the Wilderness and Spotsylvania cost both sides dearly. More than 35,000 Union soldiers were killed, wounded, or missing. Confederate losses were estimated at about 18,000. The above shows the Battle of the Wilderness.

Union soldiers used mortars to bombard the Confederate lines. The largest of these guns could hurl a 220-pound missile larger than a basketball a distance of two and a half miles.

Breastworks made of stone, soil, or timber were sometimes constructed to protect soldiers from incoming fire. This photograph by Matthew Brady shows a Union battery lined up in breastworks at the Battle of Virginia, 1864.

Surprisingly, Union and Confederate soldiers often gathered together after a day of battle. Soldiers traded food, coffee, tobacco, and other useful items between the lines.

Every week, thousands of letters passed through the post office at the Headquarters of the Army of the Potomac (top). The U.S. Mail Service (bottom), which served the Union Army, was reliable; the Confederate Postal Department, however, was sometimes a source of great frustration to Confederate soldiers and their families.

Almost every soldier sent letters home. The letters tended to focus on the daily routine of army life, with its endless hours of marching and drilling. Here, Union soldiers read letters and play cards to pass the time during the siege of Petersburg, Virginia.

57   58

Augusto 20th 860 the 6 pensyl vania war atacted By 15 of mosbays grilers 2 Bilde 2 wanded 5 prison ande now Closs on Hour side the rute flede in all Diection this is prince willians country (V. a.) ⸗

Auguste 21st 863 on pickite nof the Division wagons wente to Bristo Station ande on there returnd war capturde By mosby 3 mils from the pickite 1 sargente & five meen a ade the tearm ande Driver was all takin Bute the sargente relaste after takinge 25 sollars in money from

Hive one of the gardes ande the mail Boy was on a Heade Ande escaped capture Bute said the kesta takinge in this morning Beinge the 20 Captin with 60 men wente in search of Mosbey ande gange one Hour afterwards sevrl voleys war Hearde in the Directiond of bax market this squade war cavoeley & Sur regens haste shortly after with 25 men on the same sovel ande after olde mosbey which makes 15 men in all the 21 ware every wrone Bute Lust in the eveninge there war a fine

Some soldiers recorded their experiences in journals. The above entry is from the journal of William Cline, a soldier in the Union Army, and describes the day-to-day movements of his unit.

182

A jonah, the ill-fated fumbler found in every company, angers his fellow soldiers by spilling their coffee, dousing their fire, and wasting their meager rations.

Bad coffee and lack of food were common complaints among the soldiers. Here, a group of Union soldiers lines up for a serving of soup.

About 600,000 Union and Confederate soldiers lost their lives in the Civil War, which resulted in the end of slavery and a more powerful federal government.

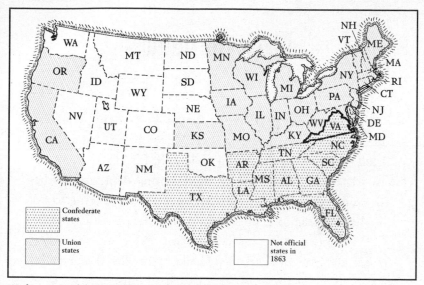

Modern map of the United States, showing the location of Virginia, as well as which states were Union and which were Confederate in 1863.

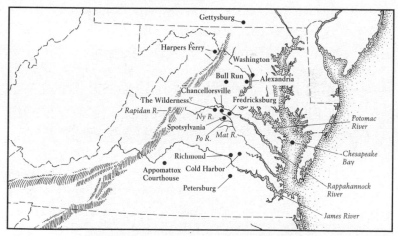

This map includes the sites of several significant Civil War battles, including Gettysburg, Petersburg, Bull Run, and Cold Harbor.

About the Author

Jim Murphy confesses that he never found the Civil War very interesting when he was in school. "The politicians and generals all seemed to write in the same stiff, florid style, and the war was always described in overly complex military terms. Then one day, while researching another book, I came across the diary of a soldier, Elisha Stockwell, Jr.

"My first surprise was to learn that he had enlisted when he was just fifteen. Until then I had never realized that someone so young had been a part of such an important event in American history. My next surprise was how much I enjoyed his writing. He was direct, honest, wonderfully detailed, and very, very funny. Even at the worst of times, he always seemed to find something humorous about the situation.

"In preparation for writing this journal, I went back and reread Elisha's diary. I also read the journals of Thomas Galway, who enlisted in the Union Army when he was fifteen and rose in rank to first lieutenant, and Benjamin C. Rawlings, who was the first Virginia volunteer for the Confederacy, at age fifteen, and had been promoted to the rank of captain by the time of Appomattox. Each of these boys had unique and exciting Civil War experiences and were witnesses to many unusual events on and off the battlefield. In addition, each lived through the frightening experience of being routed by an enemy charge and finding himself trapped behind enemy lines. Inspiration for James Pease's encounter with Sally and subsequent escape through enemy lines are based on a real incident involving a nineteen-year-old lieutenant from Missouri, George W. Bailey."

Jim Murphy is the author of over thirty-five award-winning books for children. His many critically acclaimed titles include *The Great Fire*, a Newbery Honor Book, a NCTE Orbis Pictus Award winner, and a Boston Globe–Horn Book Honor Book; *Across America on an Emigrant Train*, a NCTE Orbis Pictus Award winner; *Truce: The Day the Soldiers Stopped Fighting*, a NCTE Orbis Pictus Recommended Title; *The Crossing: How George Washington Saved the American Revolution*; *Savage Thunder: Antietam and the Bloody Road to Freedom*; *Blizzard!: The Storm that Changed America*; *The Real Benedict Arnold*; *A Young Patriot*; *An American Plague: The True and Terrifying Story of the Yellow Fever Epidemic of 1793*, which received the Sibert Medal, a Newbery Honor, and was a National Book Award finalist; and SCBWI Golden Kite Award winners *The Boys' War* and *The Long Road to Gettysburg*. His books often appear on innumerable best book lists from organizations and journals such as the *American Library Association*, *Publishers Weekly*, *School Library Journal*, and *Booklist*.

Mr. Murphy lives in Maplewood, New Jersey, with his wife, Alison Blank, two sons, and their seven-month-old puppy.

Acknowledgments

Grateful acknowledgment is made for permission to use the following:

Cover art by Michael Heath | Magnus Creative.

Interior illustrations copyright © 1998 by Jim Murphy.

Page 175 (top): Union soldier, Library of Congress.

Page 175 (bottom): Recruiting poster, ibid.

Page 176: Enlistment forms, National Archives.

Page 177 (top): Mass drill, Library of Congress.

Page 177 (bottom): Meade's Gettysburg headquarters, ibid.

Page 178 (top): M1861 Rifle Musket, Armed Forces History Division, National Museum of American History, Smithsonian Institution, Photo No. 37692-C.

Page 178 (bottom): The Battle of the Wilderness, Library of Congress.

Page 179: Union soldiers with mortars, ibid.

Page 180 (top): Breastworks, National Archives.

Page 180 (bottom): Soldiers, ibid.

Page 181 (top): Post office, Army of the Potomac, Library of Congress.

Page 181 (bottom): U.S. Mail Service, ibid.

Page 182 (top): Union soldiers, National Archives.

Page 182 (bottom): Union soldier's journal, Department of Special Collections, Hesburgh Libraries of the University of Notre Dame.

Page 183: Jonah drawings by Charles W. Reed from *Hardtack and Coffee or The Unwritten Story of Army Life*, by John D. Billings, George Smith & Co., Boston.

Page 184 (top): Union soldiers lining up for soup, Library of Congress.

Page 184 (bottom): Dead soldier, ibid.

Page 185: Maps by Heather Saunders.